QUARANTINE

DON'T COME OUT TO

COVID-19

KD STORM

Published by Books by Storm
Edited by Marni MacRae (author of *Lady Sun* and *Nameless*)
Written by KD Storm

Library of Congress Catalog Card Number 2020906527
ISBN 978-1-7331389-4-9
www.KdStorm.com
Manufactured in the United States of America

ABOUT THE AUTHOR

KD Storm was born in New York City, the hardest hit city in the United States  by COVID-19. He grew up in an immigrant household and remembers a saying from his father, Ibrahim, "Once the dust of the United States settles on the hem of your pants, you'll never want to live anywhere else again."

Ibrahim shared the story of his coming to America in the early 70's, a story KD hopes to write about one day. His father told him, "When I arrived, Uncle Ashraf guaranteed that I'll never want to leave the states, and he was right." Like many other immigrant stories, Ibrahim made it to the United States with less than ten dollars in his pocket, responsible for bringing his young sister-in-law with him on a journey that took nearly a week.

KD's father passed away in April of 2019, a year prior to the writing of this book. This book is dedicated to his memory and that of Uncle Ashraf, who always envisioned a successful career in writing for KD.

GETTING CAUGHT UP IN COVID'S STORM

Halfway through my second book, the Coronavirus took social and traditional media by Storm. How could I continue to pay attention to the book in progress while the world was talking, and panicking, about COVID-19? I couldn't. I ignored the seriousness of the virus while engrossing in the excitement of the impending apocalypse, necessary fuel for the new book. I started taking notes on the idea for Quarantine. As the days rolled by, I worked less and less on the initial book, and more and more on Quarantine.

Seeing the images of people hoarding and fighting over toilet paper and emptying out supermarkets added to the motivation for the book. Once busy highways empty during rush hour and abandoned shopping centers spurred my imagination. Many people showed another side of themselves, even though things were still relatively well in our country. I could only imagine how people would react if our basic needs were actually threatened, when stores would be emptied without being restocked, when power wasn't provided, when water stopped flowing from our pipes, when things would no longer be the way they once were.

Two months later, Quarantine was born.

'For man, when perfected,

is the best of animals,

but when separated from law and

justice,

he is the worst of all...'

~ Aristotle

'A man whose intellect prevails over

his desires is better than the angels,

whilst a man whose desire prevails over

his intellect is worse than the animals.'

~ Ali

QUARANTINE

"Where are you going?" Sadaka yelled.

"Didn't you hear that? It sounded like an explosion," Caleb replied.

"Caleb! You can't go out!"

Caleb ignored Sadaka's command and found his excuse to go outside, even if it was for a moment. The booming sound was followed by the brightness from the flames, which competed against the backdrop of the dark skies above Elk Grove Boulevard. A ball of smoke rose above the flames and disappeared into the night sky.

"What the hell happened here?" Caleb said.

His eyes settled on a man standing in his driveway a few houses down, watching the entertainment as well. His attention diverted from the flames to Caleb.

"Shouldn't you be indoors?" the man asked.

"Yeah, shouldn't you be in yours?"

Both men realized they saw one another, both men were concerned about what was happening in the shopping center on the corner of Elk Grove and Franklin Boulevard, and both men were suspicious about the other possibly informing authorities. *What if he calls and tells on me? Should I call the police before he does, or should I leave it alone—I'm sure he will too, since we were both out. If he tells, I'll tell.* The man walked slowly back to his home, looking the other way at the scene, then back at Caleb.

"Get in here!" Sadaka whispered angrily. "You're gonna get in trouble. Get inside!"

As bad as she wanted to slam the door in frustration, she left it open a crack. She didn't want to alert other neighbors because they might see her husband outside. Caleb took in the night sky directly overhead on his way back. The stars were bright, and the moon nearly full. The cool breeze caressed his face like the hands of a comforting angel. He could've enjoyed the same view from his backyard, but it wasn't the same, not since the quarantine. Tell a man to come out and spend more time outdoors, and he won't. He'll busy himself with tasks and chores until the night. Tell the same man he can't come outside, that he must stay indoors, and he'll ache to go outside.

Caleb was proud that he was able to spot the Little Dipper, despite not knowing anything else about it or how it aids in navigation. He approached the door and looked back at the neighbor a few houses down. The man had already entered his home, and Caleb was dragged by the arm into his. The door slammed shut. Sadaka threw her hands over her mouth.

"You think anyone heard?" she asked.

"I don't care. I can't take this anymore. They're gonna have to figure something out. I can't do this quarantine thing anymore. I have to go out and get some air."

"Go to the backyard. People don't mind that, they don't say anything. Why do you have to keep going out from the front?"

"Because, I feel like ripping my shirt off. I feel like I'm in jail in my own home."

"Honey, relax. I know how you feel. But this is only temporary, just until spring arrives."

"Spring? You know how long that is? Another month!"

"Honey, I know. We're all in the same boat—everyone, not just you and I."

"I wanna move. I don't wanna be here anymore. Other cities aren't doing the same thing."

"All of the major cities have some kind of restriction. Where you gonna move to? Galt? I'll suffocate and die of boredom."

"That's how I feel staying here," Caleb said. "I have to look into something else. I gotta call Wali and see what kind of homes are out there, see what we can afford."

"Then, you'll have to go by yourself. I'm not moving that far from my work and family."

"It's a fifteen-minute ride. What do you mean that far?"

"It's not fifteen-minutes. It's like an hour."

"Tracy is an hour, not Galt. Stop exaggerating."

"I'm not moving. Everything will be back to normal in a month. Just relax. Go outside in the backyard. Actually, it's better if you don't. We've made enough noise today. We don't need to add to it. I don't know who might've seen you already. Last thing I need is for the police to take you away."

"They can't take me anywhere. It's not like I'm sick."

"Yea, but they'll take you to jail if you keep going out. What do they call it—a public, what was that?"

"Public risk."

"Yeah, public risk. You know, they can take people away for that."

"Oh, God help me," Caleb said with his head raised to the ceiling. He headed straight for the patio door to the backyard, grabbed the handle, and pulled. It was locked.

"Why don't you just stay indoors tonight? Don't take any chances."

"I haven't seen any of my friends or family since November. Doesn't that bother you? Hell, I even miss my coworkers. I miss going to work. I never thought I'd say that."

"Yes," Sadaka replied. "Of course it does. I'm the one who doesn't want to move because of family."

"Then why are you acting like it's no big deal?"

"Think about all the people who celebrate Christmas, and Thanksgiving each year. Think about how they feel not being able to share those special days with their loved ones anymore. Suicide rates have gone up. When I think about my situation, and then I think about others, I don't feel that bad anymore. It's not like the government is doing this for fun, or to control us, or any other reason. It's for our own protection. If you go out and get sick, you won't even know. You'll come back and get us sick, me and Pari. And you think she'll survive if she gets the virus?

Let's turn on the news and see what's going on. Maybe we need a reminder of what's happening in the world."

"Oh yea," Caleb remembered. He ran to the living room and threw himself into the couch. He didn't want to miss what just happened a few blocks away from his home. Caleb took the local news channel. The only thing playing on television was a Family Feud re-run and home shopping network style programs. He heard a helicopter flying overhead. Caleb looked out the patio door and saw a helicopter circling around the same area where the explosion took place.

*"Earlier tonight…"*Julissa Ortiz, a reporter from Channel 31 news said.

"About time. Sadaka, come and listen. They're talking about what's happening over there."

Sadaka rushed to the living room and plopped herself where Caleb sat.

"Get out of my spot."

"Quick, sit down next to me and keep me warm," she said.

"Another Amazon truck was attacked and its driver killed by a group of bandits on the corner of Elk Grove and Franklin Boulevard. This is the second attack in a month amidst a series of attacks happening throughout the greater Sacramento area by the homeless. This is the forty fifth attack of an Amazon truck this year in the United States, and the one hundred and first of all delivery trucks," Julissa said. *"Matt, what do you think needs to happen? I mean, not only are those poor drivers, who are working so hard and putting themselves at risk of contracting the virus, bringing us the goods we need, but now they're being attacked by a different enemy."*

"Julissa, you're right. People are waiting on deliveries of important medicine and supplements to help keep their immune

systems strong against the Coronavirus, food—I mean life-saving supplies are on these trucks. But, first, let's talk about the attackers. I want to make it clear that we are using the word homeless to refer to these folks, but they're not the homeless we're accustomed to hearing about. These are people who have chosen to live a 'home-less' life because they choose not to be quarantined at home. The bulk of these 'home-less' groups are youngsters in their upper teens to 30's," Matt Pacini, a law enforcement specialist, explained. *"These bandits, earlier this evening, used spike strips on a turn that caused the truck to lose control and crash into the corner of a Jamba Juice."*

"What caused the explosion?" Julissa asked.

"The truck's fuel tank exploded as the bandits set the truck on fire after taking everything from the truck. This is also the

first murder of a delivery driver, despite all the attacks on delivery trucks."

"Matt, is it true the driver was beaten after he tried to defend the truck?"

"Yes, Julissa. That's what we were told. A simple truck driver died a hero tonight in Elk Grove. Delivery drivers, like medical staff, supermarket workers, and like ourselves, are on the frontlines of this new war we are facing."

Julissa's eyes sparkled. She became emotional. *"Look at us,"* she pointed to herself and Matt. *"We're all human beings in the same situation. After our reports, we have to rush home with escort vehicles trailing us, but we don't have a problem with it. It's just something that has to be done. If everyone were to follow instructions and orders that are designed to keep us safe, none of this would be happening."*

"I don't think the people who need to hear this message are listening, Julissa."

"You're right, Matt. The people who I'm talking to are outside. But those people who are now running the streets were once in their homes and watching TV, just like you are," she pointed to the camera. *"To those of you out there who may be thinking about the same thing, it's not worth it. The quarantine won't last forever, and once we find a treatment for this virus, things will return to normal. But, what will the criminals and murderers do? What life will you turn to when everything goes back to the way it was? This is Channel 31 news. Have a good night, because you still can."*

***

The next morning, the Douglas' mail was set in front of their door, and the bell was rung by the delivery worker. Caleb opened the door, picked up the bag, and waved at the delivery driver. He looked over to his neighbor's house, the one who saw him last night. No one was out, except for the delivery woman who hopped back in her truck.

"You know what's crazy?" Caleb asked Sadaka.

"What?"

"I've been trying to get my job to allow us to telework, telling them how much it can benefit the environment, save on utility bills, save the employees gas money which is like giving us a raise and boosts morale, saves the roads, decreases our chances of getting into accidents, gives us more personal time instead of wasting that time commuting—all that stuff. They could even save on their lease by getting enough people to telework that they can shut down a location or two. They kept delaying and not allowing it until everyone's hand was forced by the virus," Caleb said as he fired up his laptop.

"I know what you mean. Same thing with my company. We're having so many issues, and it's been a year since the Coronavirus. Every now and then, a couple of managers have to go into the office and call for escort service," Sadaka said.

Caleb was on the phone with a stakeholder. He ran the mouse with one hand and clicked away, looking for an email, while talking about other things with the person on the line.

"Njeri, how do you feel about our governor being the first in the nation to order the quarantine?" Caleb asked.

"I like that he's very proactive, but I'm not sure how I feel about the quarantine. I mean, it's been going on for four months, a complete and total shutdown. How has your family been handling the quarantine?" Njeri asked.

"We've been ok. My wife gets the escort service. It kinda makes us feel special," he laughed. "But, it's crazy. I thought last year was bad and this would all end in the summer, but the virus came roaring back. I'm still in shock and don't know if I'll ever get over this – ,"

"Wait, what? Escort service?"

"Yea. If you're an essential service provider, the police department sends a driver to you and their car escorts your car to where you need to go. She's a manager at the Employment Development Department where they cut the unemployment checks. We know that's essential."

"Right," Njeri laughed. "Everyone needs their paycheck. Tell her to get to work on time because my son is unemployed too," she said as they laughed.

Suddenly, Caleb heard noises outside. His chickens were alarmed by the sounds of people.

"Njeri, could you hold on? I need to check on something."

"Sure," she said.

Caleb looked out the front door peephole. He saw a few people walking in the street but couldn't make out who they were. Then he saw three police cars, one slowly following another.

2

Caleb opened the door.

"Get back inside," an officer passing in front of the house wearing an N-95 mask pointed.

Caleb shut the door and looked out from the window. Sadaka joined right beside him.

"What's going on?" she asked.

"No clue."

They watched as three officers on foot patrol were followed by three police cars and a full-sized blue SUV. The blue SUV's were used to carry those with COVID-19 to a hospital.

"Someone in our neighborhood has the virus?" Sadaka asked.

"I think so." They kept looking.

One officer turned to the fifth house, followed by another.

"No way," Caleb said. "They're going into that house. That's the house of the guy who was outside with me last night."

"WHAT?"

"Shhh, what's wrong with you?" Caleb said.

"Wrong with me? You were the one outside. If the cops arrest him, he might turn you in; snitch on you for being out with him. Then they'll think you also have the virus."

"Stop talking crazy. I'm gonna keep watch to see what's going on."

"Where are you going?" Sadaka yelled.

"Would you calm down? I'm going to the living room to see what's happening, gosh."

Caleb peered out the window. He saw the three officers carrying the man out of the house. One officer held his upper body while the other two tried to control his legs. The man yelled, kicked, and cried. The officer holding his upper body began losing grip.

"What the hell? Sadaka, quick. Come and take a look."

The man finally squirmed his way out of the officer's grip and landed against the concrete pavement, back first. He coughed and rolled around in pain. The officers waited until the SUV arrived, and the driver opened the back door. The driver also had on the same mask as the police officers. The officers grabbed the man, but before lifting him, one of them asked, "Are you walking on your own, or should we carry you again?"

"I'll go. I'll go. Just give me a minute," he moaned.

The man sat up and looked around.

"Hurry, we don't have time. We don't wanna use force."

The man got up, looked at the Douglas residence, and ran off.

"Get him!" an officer yelled.

The three of them gave chase. The man looked back every few strides, breathing rapidly in panic. One officer caught up and tackled him on the sidewalk in front of the Douglas' house.

Caleb's heart pounded, not because of what he saw, but because of what that man might say. He thinks I called the police on him. He's going to tell the police I was out with him last night. Is this real? Can they really take me away for simply stepping out of my home?

The man's head was pressed against the pavement. He managed to get a look at Caleb hiding to the side of the window. Sadaka returned.

"What's going on?"

"They're taking that neighbor away, the one who was out with me last night. They're taking that poor bastard to jail or the quarantine hospital. I think they might come for me too."

"Why?" Sadaka got excited.

"Because, that guy thinks I called the police on him for being outside. Now, he's gonna tell them about me, and I'm next."

"No, I think they found out he has the virus. It's not about going outside," she said.

"I hope so."

"Njeri?" Caleb asked. He looked at the cell phone and realized the call had long been ended.

"I thought things were gonna get better and calm down. Looks like it's getting worse—feels like the *Walking Dead* or that *Revolution* show is about to happen," Caleb said. "I need to get a gun."

"Don't talk crazy. You're not getting no gun." Sadaka's phone vibrated. It was an alert about the latest COVID-19 news. Sadaka walked into the kitchen with her head down, reading the alert. "Japan has become the thirteenth nation to enforce a nationwide quarantine for 2021," Sadaka shouted from the kitchen. "Italy was the first and a bunch of other European nations did the same, just like last year," she continued.

"I thought things were getting better?" Caleb said.

"I never said they were getting better. I only said there's only a month left before our quarantine ends."

***

"There's another walker," Officer Pele said as Officer Ishmael drove.

The guy had a backpack on.

Officer Pele was a short and big fella, but quick on his feet, essential for a police officer. Officer Ishmael was the intimidator, big and tall. He liked partnering with Pele, because Pele did most of the groundwork, while Ishmael came in to clean up.

"These guys don't stop," Ishmael said. "He's walking the streets as if it's no big deal. Pele, you got this one?"

"Yeah, man. Let me at him," Pele said as he put on his protective mask.

Ishmael drove closer to the sidewalk, and Pele jumped out.

Walkers were those who disregarded the quarantine and walked around aimlessly, deliberately rejecting quarantine orders. Most walkers strayed outside of their residential neighborhood because passing in front of homes would mean phone calls to the authorities. For the police, it was hard to tell a walker from a bandit, so most were treated the same. Some criminals posed as walkers to get from one place to another. Other criminals went into hiding and came out at night to move about.

"Hey, walker!" Officer Pele called out. "Hit the ground."

"I'm not sick, man. I just need to go for a walk."

"Yeah, I know. That's why we call you walkers," Pele said as he punched the guy in the chest, sending him to the floor.

The guy sat in the grass and didn't move, clearly disappointed that his walk didn't last longer.

"Where are your boys?" Pele asked.

Ishmael got out and radioed, "We got another walker, third one for the day."

"What boys?" the guy asked.

"Don't lie. Turn over with your hands behind your head."

"I told you, I just came out for a walk."

"You're lying. Where are your boys?"

"What boys?" the guy yelled.

Pele punched the guy in the back of the head. "Yell again. Go ahead."

"Dude, I didn't do anything. Lay off me."

"I'll lay off of you alright. I got no respect for anyone who don't respect the law. But I'll be honest—it's you guys who make my job fun. There's not much to do in the winter months. Everyone's indoors, not a lot of action," Pele said as he put the guy in cuffs. "You gotta know something about the truck last night. Turn around."

"What truck?"

"Bro, don't mess with me," Pele said as he put his hand around the guy's neck.

"Pele, what's the deal?" Ishmael asked.

"He says he doesn't know anything about last night."

"I'll call the SUV," Ishmael said.

The guy panicked, "What's the SUV?"

"Where you'll go to be quarantined with the rest of the sick people," Ishmael replied.

"I told you guys, I'm not sick. If you take me there, I'll get sick for sure."

"Got no choice," Pele said.

"Take me to jail or leave me alone. You got no right to take me to the hospital."

"We'll see," Ishmael said as he radioed, "Need an SUV on Elk Grove and Fire Poppy."

"NO! Please, no!"

"Few more minutes, and this useless dirt bag is someone else's problem," Ishmael said.

"He brought weapons," the guy said frantically. "He had weapons and medical supplies. I could give you guys more information, just call off the SUV."

3

"What? Who had weapons?" Pele asked.

"Call off the SUV, and I'll talk."

Pele punched him in the head.

"Pele, easy. You'll knock him unconscious, and we won't get any information," Ishmael said. "SUV is no longer needed, I repeat, SUV is no longer needed."

"State your reason please," the operator requested.

"We're taking him to jail, not the hospital. They'll run tests at the jail."

"Confirmed. SUV request cancelled. Thank you."

"Now talk!" Pele demanded.

"Will you guys let me go?"

"You're not going to the hospital, but you are going to jail."

"Okay, the Amazon driver had some guns, and ammunition, and medical supplies. That's gold on the streets. It's getting wild out here with more and more people joining street gangs. I overheard them talking about fighting for territory, turf wars against other neighborhoods and stuff."

"Guns in the delivery trucks? Where they get the guns from?"

"I don't know, but the street gangs got them now."

"Who you with? What gang?"

"I'm solo, got no gang."

"What's your name?" Ishmael asked.

"Jason."

Pele pulled out the guy's wallet from his pocket. "Jason Cunningham," Pele said.

"Jason, how do you know about the guns?" Ishmael asked.

"The guys are cool. They don't harm us solos, as long as we stay out of their way, and as long as we do something for them."

"What did you do?"

"I got the spike strip for them."

"And where did you get that at?"

"I made it with a bunch of sharp metal, nails, wire, and tape. They gave me a box of protein bars and a few bottles of water."

"How long you been walking?" Pele asked.

"About a month."

Pele got up, and stood him up. "Where's your gun?"

"Got none."

"How do you defend yourself in the streets?"

"I told you, the gangs are cool. They got enough stuff, and ain't no solo-guy gonna try and take something from me."

"Where are these gangs hiding?" Pele continued with the questions.

"Honestly, man. I don't know. But they were inside the Raley's supermarket waiting for the truck to hit the spikes before coming out. Even though the supermarkets don't have any food or supplies, some of the gangs hide out in there."

"Yea, I guess that's bound to happen with businesses completely shut down during the quarantine," Ishmael said.

"How many of them were there?" Pele asked.

"Six guys, two girls."

"Were they cute?" Pele laughed. "Let's go. We can take you to jail now."

***

Robbie waited till 10 pm, when the seniors in her apartment would be sleeping. Before heading out, she listened to her Whats App message one more time.

"Auntie, when you leave your apartment, make a right and go straight to J street, make another right and come straight down until you see me. Call me when you turn on J Street," Angel said.

Robbie, Caleb's mother and Angel's aunt, lived alone in a senior apartment complex. She couldn't tolerate the isolation anymore. Furthermore, she didn't believe the governor about the quarantine ending on March 31st.

Robbie silenced her phone, placed it in her back pocket, and headed out. She took the stairs, as the elevator would alert security. She made it to the ground level, looked around, and headed for the hallway that led out. It was quiet and dimly lit, not to attract the bandits. Robbie slyly turned the corner and came face to face with a security guard wearing an N95 mask.

"What are you doing out of your apartment?"

"My toilet doesn't work, so I came down here to use this one. Is that okay?"

"Yes, hurry. You shouldn't be out here. Next time, call maintenance so they can fix your toilet. Now, hurry!"

"Okay, thank you."

The guard waited a few feet from the bathroom door. He saw a dark figure pass by outside. The door to the apartment complex was a glass automatic sliding door. It was locked from the inside. The guard walked up to peek out the door, being careful not to get too close, as the door would open. Unaware, Robbie kept opening the bathroom door to get a peek at whether the guard was still standing there.

She didn't see him. Robbie walked out and took a look around the corner. She saw the guard looking outside. Robbie quietly walked to the other end, right around the corner from the bathroom, and made it to the door. The sliding door opened.

"Hey!" the guard yelled. "Where are you going?"

She ran out, turned the corner, and was nowhere to be found.

"You're on your own. I ain't letting you back in here," the guard shouted.

Robbie remembered the directions Angel gave her. She didn't want to get lost by starting off going the wrong way, so she waited a minute to see if the guard would come out looking for her. After standing in the cold, she made her way back across the apartment to the initial road Angel had referred to. She turned right and walked on the sidewalk all the way down to J Street. With every step Robbie took, she looked around for attackers. Gangs hoarded together, so they would be seen and heard from further away, but the homeless were another threat.

Prior to the chaos of the quarantine, the homeless population had stayed to themselves. Since the quarantine, they'd been known for attacking and stealing from walkers. No one came out to give them money, and shops weren't open for them to buy food. The epicenter of the homeless population was in downtown. The police wouldn't patrol downtown for walkers due to the abundance of the homeless population. Downtown also didn't have much in the way of residential areas, making apartment complexes, such as the one Robbie lived in, a point of interest for criminals.

Robbie finally reached the corner of J Street, emerging from the darkness of the road her apartment was on. She turned right. J Street was lit with lights lining up both sides of the road. She felt safe, and called Angel.

"I just turned onto J Street. How far should I go?"

"Okay, if you just turned, it will be about a mile. Call me in ten minutes."

"Okay. Thank you, honey," Robbie said.

She put the phone in her back pocket and walked on, happy that she would be seeing some of her immediate family soon. She felt relieved not having to be in the dark. That's when she saw an image of a person emerging from the wall of an upcoming building. Robbie tried to remain calm. She looked across the street to see if it was any safer. There was no one there. *If I go across the street, this person's going to think I'm scared and will come after me.* She walked tall, puffed her chest out, and pressed on.

"No one needs to get hurt," the voice said. "Just give me whatever you have."

"Look at me," Robbie said as she continued walking, pretending to be unafraid. "Does it look like I have anything? I'm not carrying anything except this bag of clothes." She opened the bag and shook it in front of him as she passed by.

"You got no food bars, or toilet paper, or anything?"

"I got this bottle of water and that's all."

"Keep your water. I got plenty of that from the water hoses around."

The shape blended back into the wall.

"Angel, where is this place of yours? It's been ten minutes, and I don't see any lights on," Robbie said in Whats App.

"Auntie, of course I won't leave my lights on. I need you to call me after ten minutes so I can come out and get you."

"Well it's been ten minutes—"

"There you are. I see you," Angel said as she put her phone away.

"Auntie, we're in here. Hurry," she waved Robbie down.

Robbie picked up her pace and finally reached Angel. She gave her a long and warm embrace.

"We have to get inside, quickly," Angel said.

Robbie entered Angel's Salon & Spa. Just as Angel was about to close the door behind her, a man shouted from across the street.

"Hey! You guys can't be in there like that. What's going on in there?"

Angel looked back—it was a guard from the Grand Sheraton across the street. It looked like he noticed more people inside the salon and was probably concerned about group gatherings.

"Don't worry," Angel yelled across the street. "We're in self-quarantine together as a family. No one else is coming. It's just my elder aunts and me."

"You're risking your own safety, and theirs, by herding the elders together. I won't report this as long as I don't see anyone else going in or out."

"Thank you," Angel said and closed the door behind her.

***

The parking lot of Wymarck Hospital looked like a tent campground. Two beds were in each unit. Heat and electricity were powered by gas generators, one to every two tents. The lot smelled like a gas station and a truck stop. The tents were full of sick people. What looked scarier was the parking lot and hospital were surrounded by barbed wire. No one was allowed in, and no one could leave, not until a doctor cleared a patient, and the patient was escorted by authorities. Most patients were grateful for getting treatment for the virus, but a few despised having to stay against their will.

"I'm better now, I can go home," Gerard, a man in his fifties said while sitting in his bed, and removing the tape that held the IV needle in his arm.

"Sir, sir," Nurse Miriam tried getting him to stop. "I need assistance at Bed fifty-one, now! We have a possible escapee."

"I'm not escaping anywhere. I'm not in jail. Last I checked, this was still the United States of AMERICA!" he yelled. "And unless I'm in jail, you can't hold me against my will," he removed the final piece of tape. Gerard grabbed on the needle, but he couldn't get himself to pull it out.

"Nurse, I need you to take this God damned thing out of my arm. It's making me sick."

"Sir, please calm down. You're not allowed to leave until the doctor gives the clearance."

"Screw the damn doctor. I've been waiting here since yesterday for the doctor to come around and give the clearance. I'm fine. Clear me and let me go home, and take this damn needle out my arm."

Two armed guards ran into the tent, one of them breathing heavily. The other went straight to Gerard.

"Sir, are you causing problems?"

The nurse appeared to bristle at the guard's confrontational approach. "We just need to get him to relax while I fix the needle in his arm and wait for the doctor to release him."

"Look at this bastard," Gerard said as he looked away from the guard, who looked like he wanted a confrontation. The second guard approached, standing behind the first one. "You guys can get the hell out of my face now."

"Then I insist you lay back down and let the nurse do her job."

"I AM letting the nurse do her job. You can get outta my face. I can see you're ready for a fight," he said, still looking away.

"You haven't seen how people like you are handled in other countries," the guard said. "You've got it good here. If it were up to me, I'd handle people like you the way the Chinese handle people there. With all this chaos, we don't have the time and patience to play games. Just do as you're told."

"Maybe you should go to China and work over there," he replied.

The nurse tried getting to his arm, but he was preoccupied with the guards. The guard noticed the nurse unable to secure his arm.

"You need to lay back and let the nurse do her job."

"And you need to lay off, and get out of here."

"I will do no such thing until you cooperate. Lay back down," the guard put his finger against Gerard's collar bone, pushing him back against the bed.

He slapped the guard's hand away. The guard moved in on him when the nurse got in between them.

"I think he's okay now. Thank you, guys. I got it from here."

The guard looked at Gerard, but he didn't look back. He looked at the nurse, and both he and Gerard saw the disappointment in her eyes. He looked back at Gerard and said, "You let me know if he causes anymore trouble. I'd love to take care of him for you."

***

"Why isn't mom responding to her Whats App?" Caleb asked Sadaka.

Sadaka rocked little Pari in her arms, putting her to sleep. "She probably hasn't checked it, yet."

"What's she busy with? She's locked inside her home. I told her. I told her she should come to our house or move in with Dina until this quarantine ends."

"Relax, honey. She's fine. She'll respond."

"Any other time I'd be relaxed. This time, things are different. It's scary out there. She's old. I'm concerned about her. She could end up sick, in the hospital, and die without us even knowing. Have you seen how busy the hospitals have been? Just pray that we don't get sick, because if we do, we'll die from the wait to be treated."

"Turn on Netflix and watch that show your coworker was telling you about, *Ten Seconds* or something?"

Caleb laughed, "*Seven Seconds?*"

"Yeah, turn that on. I wanna watch it too."

"I gotta get a hold of mom first."

Just then, a new Whats App message came in. It was from Robbie.

"Son, everything's ok. I'm with Angel and my sisters in Angel's salon."

"What? Where?"

"In the salon. God bless her. She made us beds, brought some food, and brought all of the aunts so we could be together."

"Wow! That's fantastic. I'm so happy you guys are not alone." There was a pause in the conversation. Caleb thought for a second and continued, "Mom, how did you get there?"

"She—she came and picked me up."

"Mom, how? No one's allowed to drive."

"Well, we're not allowed to congregate in her salon, but here we are. Don't worry about a thing, son. We're fine, and waiting for the day when things get back to normal so I can see you again."

"Mom," Caleb got emotional. "Don't talk like that."

"Like what, son?" she laughed.

"Like I can't see you whenever we want. We aren't seeing anyone, including each other, because we're obeying the laws so the virus doesn't spread, not because of anything else."

"I know, son. I know."

"It's just—the way you made it sound, like something forced us apart and we don't know if or when we'll see each other again. If I felt that for a second, I'd jump in my car right now and pick you up."

"You know I can't stay at your house. You guys keep all the windows shut and turn up the heat. I get claustrophobic."

"Well, I'm just glad you're not alone. Make sure you go back home if anyone there has any symptoms of being sick. It's not worth it."

"I will, son. I will. Don't worry. Love you."

"Love you too, mom."

***

The home was filled with people moving to and fro, each busy with a separate task. One took objects out of boxes, and threw the empty delivery boxes in the backyard. Another arranged the objects by size on the floor and countertops, while another wiped them clean. Handguns, rifles, and shotguns were scattered all over the tables and floors.

"Set one of each in every bag," a male voice said to one of the teens as he pointed to the guns on the floor and backpacks in the closet.

4

Sadaka was on her way home with a law enforcement escort vehicle trailing her. The highway was empty, and it was 4:30pm. She enjoyed the open roads, going as fast as she wanted despite the patrol car behind her.

At one point, the trailing police officer used the megaphone to announce that she needed to slow down. When she got home, the officer had warned her that anyone else might've thought she was trying to get away.

Sadaka approached the road to her house, but it was blocked off by two police cars. The trailing patrol car shot out in front of her and cut her off. Officer David Quaid signaled for Sadaka to stay back while he went to retrieve information. Officer Quaid's been providing escort service to Sadaka from downtown to her house for the past couple of months. He got out of the car to talk to the officer who stood on guard at the end of the road. "You guys got an inspection going on?" David looked at the name on her badge.

Sadaka rolled her window down to overhear the conversation as a freight train rolled through the wildlife refuge behind her.

"Yes," Officer Soraya replied. "We're going through this neighborhood today."

"Okay, because I have a State employee with me."

"I see. Which home is she in?"

"That one over there," David pointed.

"That area's been cleared. She's gonna have to wait until the medics report back."

Sadaka got upset. *Why did I have to wait? Why couldn't I simply go home? Actually, Sadaka felt entitled.* She was eligible to the escort service, as her job in the EDD was listed as an essential service. She felt she should be respected, just as much as police officers and other emergency personnel. *Why then is that officer being so brash? Why won't she move the cones aside, thank me for my service, and allow me to go home?*

"Is there a way for us to check her temperature instead of having her wait till the medics get back?" Officer Quaid advocated for Sadaka.

"I'm not a medic, Officer—"Soraya looked at David's badge to get his last name. "Quaid."

"I figured we didn't need to be a medic to take a temperature," David replied.

"You can tell her to park the car right there and that she'll have to wait until the neighborhood is cleared."

Sadaka threw her hands up in disbelief, and slammed them on the steering wheel.

"How long do you think that will be?" Officer Quaid asked.

Sadaka noticed Officer Soraya becoming impatient with the questions from Officer Quaid.

"Depends," Soraya replied. "If they don't find anyone, and everyone answers their doors right away, it could be a half hour. Any delays during the process adds more time, perhaps up to a couple of hours."

"Couple of hours?" Sadaka shouted.

Both officers turned to Sadaka in her car after hearing her shout.

Officer Quaid took in a deep breath and headed for Sadaka's vehicle. "I need you to pull the car over there," David pointed. "You'll have to wait there until a sweep of your neighborhood is complete. It can take about an hour or so."

"Why can't I go home?"

"They have to inspect you before you do, and the medics are on the other side of your neighborhood."

"This is ridiculous. Ok, I'll just let my husband know. Thanks."

Nearly two hours had passed before Sadaka paid attention to the time again. She was tired of looking down at her phone, playing spades, watching boring Snaps of people in their homes, and What's Apping friends and family. Sadaka put on her mask and got out of her car to find out how much longer she'd have to wait.

"Hi, officer. It's getting late, and I need to be home. I was told I'd have to wait about an hour, and it's been two hours."

"I told the officer it could take up to two hours," Officer Soraya replied. "Make sure to keep some social distance between us."

"Right," Sadaka stepped back. "It's been two hours. Don't you think you could let me go home, and have a medic check me when they return?"

"No, that's not protocol. If you're sick, you could get your whole family sick."

"What protocol? It's not against the law to let me go home. It's that house right there," she pointed to the same home Officer Quaid pointed to.

"Yeah, you're going to have to wait till they return." Officer Soraya's radio sounded. "I have to get this," she said. Office Soraya walked away and talked to the person on the other line. The sweep of Sadaka's neighborhood was nearly complete, with no one showing any signs of the virus. She noticed the officer had finished her call and stayed where she was, probably to avoid Sadaka.

"Any news?" Sadaka asked.

"No. You'll just have to wait in your vehicle," she said abruptly.

"I don't understand why you can't let me go home. It's as if we're making up rules as we go along. It's not against the law for me to go home," Sadaka became agitated.

"Ma'am, back in your car please!"

"The hell with that," Sadaka mumbled as she stormed back to her car. She rolled up her car window and locked the door. She thought about her next move for a second. *What's the big deal about going home? It's understandable if I can't take the car past the cones until the sweep is complete, but stopping me from going home? These rules are ridiculous. I need to get home to my baby, and to eat.* Her grumbling stomach agitated her anger. She headed home on foot.

"Where you going?" Officer Soraya asked.

"I'm going home," Sadaka said.

"No you're not," Officer Soraya stepped onto the sidewalk.

Sadaka kept her pace.

"You need to slow down, ma'am."

Sadaka ignored the police officer and walked around her. Officer Soraya grabbed Sadaka's arm.

"Let go of me!"

"You can't pass these cones. What do you think you're doing?"

"Going home! I'm doing as the governor ordered, going home and staying home."

"No, you're not," Officer Soraya came face to face with Sadaka. Soraya gritted her teeth, looked Sadaka in the eyes, and said through her mask, "You're going back to your car."

"Leave me alone, okay," Sadaka pulled her arm away.

She continued toward home when Officer Soraya tackled her from behind onto a lawn.

"What are you doing?" Sadaka yelled. She couldn't believe what was happening. "Get the hell off me!" Sadaka shouted.

The medics turned the corner, back to where Officer Soraya was stationed. They were followed by three police officers and two patrol vehicles. The officers noticed the situation, and two of them ran to Soraya's aid.

"Get off of me!" Sadaka shouted.

Officer Soraya got on top and punched Sadaka during the struggle. She punched again, striking Sadaka on the side of her face.

"Calm down," Officer Soraya said as she struggled to grab Sadaka's arm. The other officers arrived, fell on each side of Sadaka, and restrained her. They turned her around while Officer Soraya cuffed her from behind.

"Ouch, my wrist."

One of the officers noticed the excessive tightness of the cuffs. He looked at Soraya but didn't say anything.

"What's going on here?" the officer asked.

"She's trying to get home. I told her she had to wait till you guys got back, but she insisted."

"I waited in my car for two hours," Sadaka yelled. "My house is right there, RIGHT THERE, but she wouldn't let me go home."

The officer looked at Officer Soraya again. He turned to Sadaka, "Ma'am, we're just following orders. What are you doing outside anyway?"

"I'm getting off work. I release the checks to your unemployed family members. I was escorted here and was left to wait for God knows how long."

"What now?" the officer asked Soraya.

"I don't know. We could take her to the station for resisting arrest," Officer Soraya said but thought about a better idea. She wanted to make Sadaka's day as miserable as possible for putting her through this.

"Medic," Officer Soraya yelled. "Come here and do a quick temperature check."

Sadaka was concerned. "Wait. My temperature's gonna be high. You just beat me up."

"Then we take you to the clinic for precautionary measures," Officer Soraya grinned.

"Well, let's take your temperature too," Sadaka said. "If I've got anything, I definitely passed it on to you," Sadaka grinned back.

"It's up to you. You can either let us take your temperature, or I can take you to the station and arrest you for resisting arrest."

"Resisting arrest? You weren't arresting me. You were beating me up. What law did I break, officer?" Sadaka turned to the one who appeared reasonable. "I was following the governor's orders by trying to go straight home. I was in my car, out here for over two hours—"

"It wasn't over two hours. It was barely that long—"

"Two hours, officer. I didn't break any laws to be put under arrest. I've been law abiding my whole life. Officer Soraya seems like she's having a bad day—"

"Temperature or station?" Officer Soraya yelled. "Pick one. Your choice."

5

Caleb couldn't wait any longer. He came out of the house and saw the commotion taking place not long after Sadaka sent him a text saying she was walking home.

"Hey, go back inside!" a medic shouted.

"I'm looking for my wife. She just sent me a message saying she was coming home, from there," Caleb pointed toward the police at the end of the road.

One of the officers heard the medic and saw Caleb standing outside his house. "Sir, get back inside," he yelled from the end of the road. The officer walked toward Caleb, yelling and pointing, "Sir, back inside the house."

"I'm waiting for my wife. Do you guys have her? Is that...? Sadaka? Sadaka!" Caleb called out as he headed down the sidewalk and came face to face with the officer.

"Sir," the officer put a hand on Caleb's chest, breathing heavily through his mask. "You need to go back inside."

"I need to find out what's going on with my wife. She just got off work and was on her way home."

"Sir, I'm not in the mood," the officer shoved him.

"Neither am I. Our daughter is crying, I've been cleaning the house, and working from home all day. I'm exhausted and need her help."

The officer kept his hand to Caleb's chest while Caleb looked over his shoulder.

A medic ran to Sadaka with a temperature gun. He took her temperature, showed it to the police, and headed for a minivan parked on the side of the road by the police cars. Most of the medics got inside and took off. Two of them waited by the police cars awaiting instruction from the officers. A blue SUV was parked in front of the minivan. Caleb watched as two officers grabbed Sadaka by the arms and dragged her toward the truck.

"What are you guys doing?" Caleb yelled.

"Your wife has a fever. They're taking her just to make sure."

"A fever? She's been fine. She's not sick. Hey!" Caleb shouted to the officers who dragged away his wife off.

"Sir, I suggest you go back inside, take care of your daughter, and stay in touch with your wife till she gets back home."

"Wait!" Caleb shouted. He walked past

the officer, who grabbed Caleb's arm. Caleb wrestled his arm away and ran toward the police. Another officer drew his gun.

Sadaka shouted, "Get off of me. I don't have a fever. Caleb! They're taking me away for no reason. Get a lawyer, Caleb! Call a lawyer. They can't do this. This is still America. They can't do this."

The officer chased Caleb and jumped on his back, but Caleb didn't fall. He continued on with the officer on his back. The officer began choking Caleb from behind to get him to stop. Caleb bent over and flipped the officer off his back. The officer landed hard against the pavement reaching for the pain in his back.

"Another step and your dead!" the officer shouted. "Go ahead and test me."

Caleb saw the fury on his face. Police officers don't tolerate the abuse of one another, especially during the chaotic times since Covid.

Caleb put his hands in the air, and watched his wife getting carried off. "I'll get a lawyer. Don't worry, we'll get you out. I don't know what these bastards are up to."

"Go inside and take care of Pari. Don't worry about me," Sadaka said as she was shoved into the back of the SUV.

"I can't believe this. I can't believe what you guys are doing," Caleb said.

"Just, don't move. I don't want to kill anyone today," the officer said. "We don't need the extra paperwork."

The officer on the ground finally got up. Even though the officer was in pain, Caleb could tell the officer felt bad for him, and didn't want to make things worse. The ordeal was over.

"Let's get outta here," the officer said as he clutched onto his shoulder.

"He's gotta get back inside the house," the officer with the gun said.

"Don't worry about him. He's going back. His daughter's crying inside."

***

Officer Pele radioed to Officer Ishmael, over the radio, "I'm gonna follow some delivery trucks. I think you should do the same and see what we come up with, since we're separated today."

"Guns and weapons in the delivery trucks, what do you think is going on?" Ishmael asked.

"I don't know, but if the Guard finds out they'll be all over this neighborhood. If we make the discovery, we'll be the heroes."

"Good plan, Pele. I'm with it."

Officer Pele finally spotted a delivery truck speeding down Elk Grove Boulevard. He followed it into a neighborhood.

The truck driver kept looking back into the driver side mirror. He pulled the truck over and waved to the officer to pass him up. Instead, Officer Pele pulled over behind him.

Pele got out. "You can keep going. There's been a number of delivery truck heists in the area, and I wanted to make sure your route is safe."

"Oh. Thanks, officer, but I'll be okay. I know how to navigate the streets."

"You can continue with the deliveries so you're not late. I have orders to ensure the safety of the trucks that come through here."

Reluctantly, the driver got back on the road.

Pele radioed Ishmael, "I got another idea. I need your help. I'll let you know the addresses of the places the driver makes deliveries. You inspect the packages he drops off while I follow the truck."

"Where are you?" Ishmael asked.

"I'm following a truck on Fire Poppy."

The driver pulled over to the first home on his Elk Grove route. He pulled out two small packages, ran it up to the home, and rang the doorbell. Typically, delivery drivers rush back to their vehicles to keep up with the social distancing laws in place during quarantine and to limit the possibility of theft from the truck. Instead, Pele watched the delivery driver lift the welcome mat, look down at an envelope, look around, and drop the mat without picking up the envelope. He ran back inside the truck.

To the side of the house, Pele noticed a Gyro King food truck with its lights on. Someone went in and out of the backyard carrying food from the truck. Lights were on, and people were talking and having a good time. This blatant violation of quarantining and social distancing distracted Pele from the delivery. He went around the side of the house where the food truck was parked. A skinny young man opened the front door, picked up the packages, and looked under the mat. He picked up the envelope and took it back inside.

"Ishmael," Pele radioed. "I need you to follow the truck. I gotta check out a house—looks like they got a party going on here."

The delivery truck headed down the road, turned the corner, and was out of sight. The sun was setting, and the once blue sky incorporated hues of orange. The weather felt crisp and cool, and the family took full advantage of the evening. The sounds of laughter and talking increased as Pele made his way to the truck. The cook inside the truck looked like he'd seen a ghost when he saw Officer Pele approach.

"Hey, officer. What can I get you? I know you guys been working hard."

"Hey, what's going on here?"

"We're serving gyros, your choice of meat over rice, and our special, King Fries."

"No man, what are you guys doing here?"

"Oh, we're catering to the lovely folks who live here. They have a little gathering to celebrate the end of the quarantine."

"What's your name?"

"My name? My name is Q."

"Listen, Q. There's no way to know when the quarantine is gonna end, you feel me?"

"I got you."

"You guys can't be out here like this. Give them their food, and take off so I won't have to ticket you."

"Alright, that's fair. I appreciate that, officer. What's your name?"

"Pele."

"Thanks, Officer Pele, you're cool. You look like my brother. I appreciate your help," Q said. He turned to his assistant, who was prepping the meals. "Hurry up, fool. Get the food out so we can go. And make a King Fry special for Officer Pele."

"I'm good, guys. I'm gonna have a talk with the residents here."

"Alright, officer. Have a good day."

Across the street, Pele noticed a Sky West Realty "for sale" sign. He dialed the number of the agent, Wali.

"This is Wali."

"Wali, hi. The name's Officer Pele. I need your assistance."

"Officer? Is everything ok, or are you in the market for a house?"

"Yes, in a way. You've got a home for sale on the corner of…"

6

"The governor's vision of universal health care for all Californians was so close to becoming a reality until COVID-19 hit. Explain to us how close we actually were, and why it was stopped," Gavin from 106.5 The End asked the governor's health advisor, Doctor Rick Nuri.

"Gavin, universal coverage was pending a tax increase until late last year. The bill was introduced on November 3rd and on the governor's desk by the 23rd. COVID was around for a year at that point. It was actually COVID that pushed us

closer to universal coverage," Dr. Nuri said.

"So, I was misinformed then. I thought COVID ruined universal health care, not pushed us to it."

"Gavin, you're right. But, that's not the entire story. Getting everyone health coverage was even more essential after COVID, for obvious reasons. The tax increase proposed in the bill was overwhelmingly accepted and approved by both the people and politicians. COVID's been that much of a monster."

"Before we move on, doctor, I want to inform those who may have just checked in that I'm interviewing Dr. Nuri about COVID-19 and the collapse of universal health care. The both of us are in our own homes and interviewing remotely. Take it over, doctor."

"Thanks, Gavin. In 2020, many health plans had to pay more than what they were *bringing in due to the number of people who had to be treated and the costs of the treatments from the Coronavirus. That cost was offset by a federal stimulus package. However, the high costs are still occurring and getting worse, and the federal government can no longer afford to bail out the health plans. What that means is, in order for the health plans to survive, despite many layoffs and 'trimming of the fat,' as they said, there was an increase in the cost of the premiums."*

"Right," Gavin agreed. "That's why I saw my contribution from my paycheck more than double."

"Yes. So did I, and so did the rest of California. While you and I may still afford it and keep our health insurance, most Californians could not take a premium increase that doubled, and in some cases, tripled. So what happened? Most people with insurance, whether through Covered

California, or their employer, or direct purchase from the plans, opted out. You know what that means?"

Gavin answered, "That people like us, who still have our insurance, will see another increase?"

"Yes. Premiums are set to spike again, which will lead to even more people dropping coverage, and that cycle may lead to the collapse of the health care system as we know it, if we don't get a good handle on this virus."

"Yikes. As if things weren't scary enough out there, to add to the mess is the potential loss of health insurance."

"Covered California's director, Peter Lee, says that they'll still be around and provide financial help for those in need of insurance. Employers are still providing insurance. But when premiums are truly unaffordable..." Dr. Nuri took in a deep breath.

"*Doctor, where are we with the vaccine?*"

"*There's a vaccine coming soon. I don't know how soon, but I understand it's this year.*"

"*And there you have it. We'll call it, 'the potential collapse of health insurance and the definite collapse of universal health care.' Doctor, one more thing to clarify or reiterate—this is also the potential collapse of health insurance providers.*"

"*Yes. If no one is buying health insurance and most people are going without health coverage, companies such as Blue Shield, Anthem, etcetera, may no longer be around.*"

"What about Kaiser?" Gavin asked.

"*Kaiser's unique in that they are also a health care provider, so they are sticking around as long as someone pays them for doctor and hospital visits. At the end of the day, if the money isn't there, the service*" *won't be available."*

"Thank you so much for your time, Doctor Nuri. This is Gavin signing off from my home, from 106.5 The End."

***

Pari fell asleep on the couch. Caleb pulled the little blanket over her legs to weigh them down so she doesn't jerk herself awake. He lowered the TV volume and went into the shower with his phone. "Hi, I'm looking for a lawyer who's willing to take on a case where the police and medics took my wife away, saying she had a fever when she hadn't," Caleb said.

"Why, then, did they take her away? What was the reason?" the attorney's screener asked.

"Honestly, I don't know. But I know for sure she didn't have a fever. She wasn't sick when she left for work. Almost everyone at her job teleworks—she said something about the cop being rude to her. When I went outside to see what was going on, I was stopped by two officers, while the others dragged her off into the truck like some criminal. It's like we're living in some Communist country or something."

"Honestly, there doesn't seem to be much good news. This is not a case anyone will take. It requires further investigation against law enforcement, which no lawyer that I know has the time to do, not since the chaos started last year. We've been overloaded with cases of people who haven't been sick but contracted the virus after being exposed in hospital settings. Nurses, doctors, and other medical staff are suing their former employers after coming down with mega-doses of the virus by not being given the proper protective gear to treat patients. Not everyone who goes into these hospitals has the Coronavirus, but nearly everyone who comes out has it. These people go in clean and come out with the virus, passing it on to others."

"What are you saying?"

"I'm saying, find out where your wife is and get her out of there before she gets the virus."

Caleb turned the knob that was covered in years of soap scum, and water poured from the showerhead. The water was cool, so was the night, and so was the house. It gave him goosebumps. "I can't believe this," he mumbled. "Why would they take her?" He waited for the water to warm up while he thought about what those bastards could be doing to his wife. He pointed the shower head away, but cold gusts from the cool water made him shiver. "Why's this water not getting warmer?" Caleb turned the faucet completely to hot. The water usually boiled over immediately—not this time. He took a quick, short, and incomplete shower.

***

"Angel, isn't there a working heater here?" Robbie asked.

"I don't know what happened. We have central heat, but I don't know why it stopped working."

"The Day of Judgment is here," Aunt Dawn said in her relaxed tone.

"This is nothing," Aunt Katie said in her bold and confident voice as she assisted Angel in preparing breakfast.

Angel had a few cans of propane, a portable stove top, a pan, and fresh eggs. Two chickens clucked around in the back room kicking and scratching at shredded wood only to find tile floor. Still, they pecked at the ground in the hopes of finding food.

Angel and her husband, Mike, had gotten the idea of raising backyard chickens last year from Caleb. Caleb had decided to get a few chickens after the first statewide shelter-in-place orders. Last summer, after a short lift of the orders, Mike had decided to get a few for their own yard. When Angel came to the salon, she'd brought two of them with her. Mike and the kids were still in the process of packing essentials before joining Angel at the salon, after threats of violence and drive-by vandalism took place at their residence from random people. Angel suspected it to be Mike's debt collectors, but no one knew for sure.

Aunt Katie continued, "Do you think that Heaven will be yours without being tested like those before you?" Her sisters were listening. Katie knew she had their attention. "We still have food, medicine, shelter, and to some extent, security. People back in the day didn't have half of what we still have, and it was the norm." She paused a moment, and continued, "Half the world's population still doesn't have what we have. Children are drinking from infested rivers with barely any clothes on their back, freezing to death in the winters and dying of thirst in the summer. We have nothing to complain about!"

"That's true," Robbie said as their fourth sister, Kadija, nodded. "I just pray that I never see any of my children die before me. That's my only request," Robbie said.

"Selfish! What about us?" Katie said.

"I make this prayer for all of us, for all mothers."

Robbie looked at Kadija and lowered her eyes. She just remembered Kadija's son had died a few years back.

Kadija took in a deep breath. Then she began, "Pray and never stop praying, but don't forget what Katie just said. Many mothers had their children pass away before them. There's no guarantee for any of us, and your sister is evidence," Kadija said, referring to herself. "Do your best to build yourself up mentally to be ready for anything that comes our way—anything!"

Angel brought over a pan filled with popping hot oil and eggs for everyone to eat. Katie carried the bread and broke off a piece to eat on the way. Kadija felt guilty about being served by her older sister, so she got up to bring the tea. As soon as they settled to enjoy breakfast, someone pounded on the glass door. Everyone froze with food in their mouths. All of the windows and doors were boarded up from the inside.

Angel remembered Mike's frustration at the quality of work from the day laborers she hired.

"Why didn't you have them put the boards on the outside?" Mike asked Angel when he first saw the boards. "The purpose of the boards is to protect the windows."

"You should've told me before. We don't have any more money to have them come back and redo the job. It'll be fine," Angel said.

"I know there's people in there," the guy continued pounding on the glass door. "This is the third day in a row, and the smell of your breakfast is killing me. I want some," he said.

"Uh, there's no one in here except me and my husband. We have a gun," Angel's voice shook. "I think you should find another place to have breakfast."

"Either way, you'll be doing me a favor. Kill me, and end this horrible world for me, or feed me. I'm going to start tapping against the glass door with my crowbar. It'll continue getting louder until you let me in, or the glass breaks."

Tap, tap, tap, the tapping got harder each time.

"Leave us alone, stupid!" Robbie yelled.

"Oh, so it's only you and your husband? I don't even think he's in there. Maybe out scavenging, like I am."

Tap, tap, tap!

"He's going to break the glass," Kadija said.

"What should we do?" Robbie asked as she looked around for a place to hide.

"Don't worry. Let him come and I'll show him," Angel said. She pulled out her handgun from behind the register. "Now, let's sit down to eat," she said as she tried to calm her nerves despite the banging that continued getting louder.

Tap, tap, bang, crash! Glass fell to the floor.

"I can't believe this! What the HELL ARE YOU DOING?" Angel yelled.

The man jabbed his crowbar in between a space where two of the boards met, another boarding error as each section of glass should have had a separate board its size attached to it. He moved the crowbar left and right, creating a bigger gap with every movement. The women saw the board moving, shifting from its place. The man created enough space for his fingers. He dropped the bar, stuck his hands through, and pushed and pulled the board, ripping the corners off its screws. He slammed his shoulder into the board, creating a gap big enough to squeeze himself through. He made his way in, scraping against the wood. He picked up his crowbar and set it over his shoulder, walking relaxed and confident. Angel held the gun pointed at him. He looked away and sat next to her aunts. They all stared at him in disbelief at the lack of concern he had. He set the crowbar beside himself.

"God, the smell," Katie said as she got off the floor and moved away from him. "He's sick."

"I'm not sick. I just smell," the homeless man laughed. "I should invent a cologne and call it 'homeless'," he laughed again. "What do we have here? Tasty looking eggs, bread, and tea. This is nice."

He sat Indian style, mimicking Robbie and Kadija.

"Go ahead and eat with me," he said. "Say, what kinda bread is this? Never seen it before."

Everyone remained speechless and watched the homeless man eat their food.

"We're afraid of catching the virus, that's why we don't want anyone in here," Angel said. "Would you mind taking a plate and leaving?"

"You should lower the gun. You're not gonna shoot me, so why make your arm tired?" His eyes landed on the blankets and pillows that lined up the walls of the salon. He heard chickens clucking. "Wha?" he said with a mouth full of food. "What was that? You got chickens in here?"

No one replied.

"Looks like you guys are living like

me, sleeping on the floor. But, your beds look more cozy. Maybe I could stay with you guys."

Each person had a thick blanket folded in half and pressed against the walls as their bed. The beds were topped with a pillow and another blanket. Dawn's bed was in the furthest corner, separate from the other four. She snored the loudest so she set her bed away from everyone else.

Angel lowered the gun.

"Is that stupid corona thing still going around?" the homeless man asked. "Speaking of, I could use a nice cold Corona right now," he chuckled. Living on the streets, I'm immune to everything so I won't get sick. I don't know what's going on in the world," he said with a mouth full of food. "I don't have a TV to watch, but I have noticed more and more people living the street life with me."

"You already broke her glass, which you won't be paying for. The least you could do is take your food and let us eat in peace," Katie said.

"So, that means I can't stay? Fine! That's what you want? Fine!" The man piled on nearly all the eggs, took nearly all the bread, and picked up his crowbar. "Thanks for the food," he said as he walked out, crushing glass under his feet.

7

"Wali, your cooperation with the police department is really appreciated," Officer Ishmael said.

"No problem, no problem at all. You just let me know how else I can help. Anything I can do to help make our neighborhoods safer, I'm all in," Wali said as he clasped his hands. "You never know, maybe you'll like the house so much, you might end up actually buying it," he smiled.

"I'd doubt it," Officer Ishmael smiled back.

"Okay," Officer Pele showed Wali to the door. "We gotta set up. Remember, don't say anything to anyone about this. If you could, temporarily take it off the market. I wouldn't want anyone coming by to check out the house. And don't forget to take your sign with you."

"I'll do that, officer," Wali said with his frequent smile. "Oh, one more thing. Please help yourself to some tea or snacks or anything like that. I brought some just in case you guys might want them. I left them in the kitchen."

"Thanks," Ishmael waved.

Pele closed the door and locked it. "So this house we're staking out, these fools had a party going on in their backyard. I'm surprised no one called to report it. I mean, they even had a food truck catering to them. Can you believe that?"

"Food truck? What did they serve? I'm kinda hungry."

"They had gyros and fries and stuff. They hooked me up with fries loaded with sauces and meat. At first, I didn't want it, but when I saw it, ohh wee. It was good."

"You're making me hungry," Ishmael said.

"Anyway, I had to break up the party and get them to bring the noise down. Anyone else would've arrested someone."

"That's true."

"But I followed that delivery truck to this house. He delivered two packages, kind of small. Check this out, you know what the driver did?"

"What?"

"He lifted the mat to their front door, saw an envelope laying there, looked around, I think he might've seen me, and dropped the mat without taking the envelope. What do you think that was about?"

"We're about to find out," Ishmael said.

"No, bro. We already found out. That was a payoff that he didn't pick up because he knew he was being watched. Mystery solved. This is how fast we get things done when you got me on your team."

"We need actual evidence before making a move."

"I know, I know. I'm just saying, you can thank me later when this case is closed," Pele said.

"This delivery has gotta be tied in with the attack on that Amazon truck a few days ago, when the driver was killed. These delivery drivers have been bought off by some of these residents. They're stocking up on weapons. Ever since last year, gun stores have been emptied—everyone's getting a gun."

"These weapons aren't legal either," Pele said.

Ishmael set up the video cameras. The second story window had a view of the side of the house. One camera was pointed to capture some of the front and side of the house, the other was fixed on the backyard, overlooking the fence.

"I got it," Pele tapped Ishmael.

"You're solving case after case by sitting there and thinking. You should've been a detective," Ishmael said sarcastically." Can we get some action so we can actually take some action?"

"Damn, Izzy!" Pele said to get his attention. "Bro. This is big."

"What is?"

There's a kingpin working this operation. Hear me out. He's working to get illegal guns into the hands of anyone who wants it. Nowadays, everyone wants one. This is big business. This house that we're scoping out is just a piece of the puzzle. We have to find the head of the operation. Hopefully we'll get answers from these guys."

"You could be right, and that's a big deal. We can also add stockpiling to the charges if they have several. Stocking up on anything is illegal during quarantine."

***

"Tonight, on Channel 31 news, a massive forced evacuation and quarantine of an entire Natomas neighborhood after dozens of people tested positive to the virus," Julissa said. *"Here's some footage from earlier."*

"I don't know why I'm being taken away. I don't even have a fever. I didn't test positive. Why are they taking me away? This ain't right," a lady was escorted to the back of a truck with others suspected of carrying the virus.

"This is bull—. I ain't sick, but now, hanging out with these other folks who got the virus, I'ma get sick. I'm suing the city. This is bull—."

"As you can see, residents of this Natomas neighborhood are outraged at this order," the reporter said.

Julissa looked up out of the view of the camera, as if someone was trying to get her attention. She quickly turned back to the camera, and continued, *"Which leads me to Doctor King. Doctor King, tell us a little bit about your background."*

"Sure, Julissa. Thanks for having me. I'm a general practitioner in private practice out of Carmichael and West Sacramento. I've studied medicine for over a decade. One of my specialties is incorporating healing from the natural world, whenever feasible, such as diet."

"That's great, Doctor. It's not often that we hear about doctors incorporating the best of both worlds."

"Exactly! Now don't get me wrong, when it comes to this virus, there's only one thing that'll keep it from attacking a healthy person, and that's the vaccine. However, the healthy person, through diet and lifestyle, is the least vulnerable to

complications from this virus or any other disease."

"I'm glad you mentioned that, because I've heard the virus doesn't only go after the sick or elderly, but that it's infected and killed even the healthy."

"Sure, Julissa. What you've heard is true. But what you've heard may also be blown out of proportion. For example, did you know the seasonal flu infects and kills healthy people as well? However, the overwhelming majority of its victims are the elderly and sick. Similarly, COVID-19's overwhelming victims are the sick and elderly. Every now and then, it will pick out and take down a few healthy people. Science isn't able to explain everything. Since the infectious rate of COVID-19 is so much higher than the flu, mathematically, it will kill more of the healthy and young compared to the flu."

"What more can you tell us about our only hope—the vaccine?"

"Excellent question, Julissa. What I've heard from my circle is that the pharmaceutical company responsible for making the vaccine is teaming up with a large Silicon Valley corporation to add a kind of technology in the vaccine that will give us detailed data."

"Technology in a vaccine?"

"Yes, sounds crazy," Dr. King laughed. "Basically, we won't need thousands of hours of manpower for research, and we do need the research. The vaccine will have microscopic technology that measures several things in a patient's blood, such as the amount of vaccine remaining in their system. This is to determine when the person will need a booster. It also measures and tests whether the Coronavirus is in the blood. It can even check and monitor your blood sugar without having to poke yourself. It's like having ongoing blood monitoring without running to the lab to get poked each time."

"*You're kidding? That sounds so convenient—*"

"*And accurate, in real time,*" Dr. King added.

"*So, where is all this data stored? I mean, who gets this information? Does the patient get it, or do they have to go through their doctor?*"

"*From what I understand, there will be a main hub to monitor these stats so we can get a very real and accurate understanding of the virus. Julissa, this thing's killed so many people, we can't afford to be in the dark about it much longer.*"

"*So you're for it? I mean, for the technology in the vaccine?*"

"*I love the idea, but I'd want every American to be given the option to decide for themselves, since it's not only medicine that's being put inside us.*"

"*I could see a lot of people freaking out. Will it be able to track people? I know*" lots of people are opposed to the idea of being micro-chipped."

"I don't know the details of the technology, Julissa, but I wouldn't rule out tracking. The benefit of tracking is that we'll be able to tell where the virus is going or coming from. For example, if we can track someone, and they suddenly come up with the virus, we have a very good idea on where they could've gotten it from. But this is why I also support individual choice. I think we can get enough data from volunteers alone, but if all the vaccines for this virus have the technology within it, then it may not be left to choice."

"Yes, I've also heard that the vaccine will be mandatory."

"That's likely. The virus' impact is far too great to leave this vaccine optional. But, I don't know if the government can enforce it. It's, essentially, micro-chipping."

"Speaking of numbers, I hear all sorts of numbers regarding infectious rates, deaths, and all that. Can you shed some light for us?"

"Sure. Let's compare this virus to the flu, just so we have something to compare it to. There are two main things to consider, death and the infectious rate. The Coronavirus is, approximately, three times more infectious and three times more deadly than the flu. The flu has a global mortality rate of two hundred thousand to half a million people a year."

"Wow!"

"Right, those are numbers many people don't know about. We average approximately 30,000 deaths in the United States each year from the flu. Now, in comparison, the Coronavirus was suspected to be three times more infectious and three times deadlier than the flu. Initially, it was thought the global numbers

could jump up to three million deaths, with almost a hundred thousand in the United States alone. However, there's an unknown factor the scientific community has yet to figure out, because this year there's been over half a million deaths in the United States alone from COVID-19."

8

Caleb looked for a missed call, text message, or a Whats App message from his wife, who he hadn't heard from since being arrested yesterday. He was worried sick about her. Caleb didn't have any food since the prior evening, and breakfast is his favorite meal of the day. He stared into his daughter's eyes, seeing Sadaka's. *When was she going to be home? When will I hear from her? Where can I go to get information?* The police station hadn't returned his voicemail, the 911 operator had rudely hung up on him for calling for a non-emergency reason, and he hadn't contacted any of her family for fear worrying them.

He turned to social media.

"You guys seen the news? #CivilWar," one of Caleb's social media friends posted.

He scrolled down and saw another post, "Wo, the military's gone out of control. I thought they were defending our freedoms? Not in Natomas."

Caleb continued scrolling, looking for further information to see what was going on. For a moment, he forgot about Sadaka. Another post read, "Why isn't any of this on the local news?" Attached with the comment was a picture of two soldiers, one appears to be lifting his foot off of a civilian on the ground, while the other was aiming a gun at him.

Caleb remembered something about Natomas on television last night—Channel 31 with Julissa. But, he couldn't recall any details of the incident people were talking about. Caleb was tired and thought it might be his exhausted mind incapable of remembering the news clip from last night. He turned on the TV, going from station to station to find anything about Natomas. Two news stations were on, but none were reporting anything about Natomas—they were merely talking about the White House's actions and reactions to incidents related to the pandemic. Caleb sat back in his couch, watched the news, and tried to recall Channel 31's reporting last night. Finally, he remembered. They mentioned it, but never got into the story. The reporting was all about numbers, and that crazy vaccine idea. *They showed Natomas, but talked about the vaccine and the virus. Entire North Sacramento neighborhoods evacuated by force using military might should take over any local discussion.* Caleb got on his phone again, and post after post talked about Natomas. Videos of people being dragged on the streets, as if they were criminals or unwanted luggage by masked men in military attire and tossed into the backs of trucks were plastered all over social media. Another video showed a military officer shooting rubber bullets from a shotgun at a couple of large gym rats with no shirts on. Mothers yelled, daughters cried, men argued and tried to fight.

Another person shared a post of someone in Natomas, "We got guns and can fight back if we want to, but the mere fact that we're not going to war with them shows our cooperation. They can't simply come to our homes and drag us out to jail, or the hospital because a few of us might have the virus. They can't do this, if this is still the United States of America. They can't!"

***

Sadaka remained quiet in the back seat as Officer Soraya drove her home. Her phone had been dead since last night. "We're trying our best to keep everyone safe," Soraya said.

Sadaka stared out the backseat window, watching empty parking lots pass by, one after another. She couldn't believe how a once bustling and busy city became so barren and lifeless. As much as traffic annoyed her, she realized the beauty in life was from people. *What makes places like Times Square a global attraction are the lights and the people; the crowds. Could you imagine a Times Square without people? Who would want to visit that?* She'd seen San Francisco's Fisherman's Wharf several times on cold nights with the shops closing and visitors leaving. The Wharf lost its appeal when the crowd emptied.

"We're all living in difficult times; everyone, including police officers," Soraya continued. "We all need to work together to get through these times. The more people work with us, the more we'll be able to attend to true emergencies."

Sadaka looked into Soraya's eyes through the rearview mirror. Soraya looked back. Sadaka looked away. Her arms were folded across her chest. She continued looking outside.

Sadaka rang the doorbell. She heard Caleb's footsteps run to the door, but paused. She was happy that he remembered to first look through the peephole, but she was stressed, exhausted, and hungry. Caleb opened the door. Sadaka's face was pale. Behind her, on the road and in her car, was Officer Soraya. Sadaka saw the happiness in Caleb's face turn into a frown when he recognized the officer in the car.

"Come in, honey," Caleb said as he moved aside.

He moved in to hug her, but she kept him away with a stiff arm to the chest. "I need to take a quick nap here on the couch. I don't want to touch you or the baby, not till I'm sure."

"Sure? Didn't they test you?"

"They did, but I was on a floor with several other sick people. I'm sure most of them have the damn virus."

"Why would they take you to a place with other infected people, if they hadn't even tested you yet?"

Sadaka was too tired to carry on the conversation. Thinking about what she was exposed to was very frustrating. Anymore loss of energy might result in a fainting spell. She threw herself onto the couch in the guest room. "Honey, could you get me my pillow and a glass of water?"

"Yeah, sure. How about some food?"

"No, just water for now. Thanks, love."

"Aren't you gonna take a shower?"

"Yes, as soon as I get some energy. Don't worry, I'll sanitize the couch."

***

Headlights of a delivery truck raced down Bruceville Road. The vehicle cut through thick fog. Two guys hid behind a tree, one with a shotgun and the other with a long-range rifle. The guy with the rifle took aim, waiting for the truck to come within sight. He saw lights trying to pierce their way through the fog but couldn't see the truck. The guy realized the truck was getting ready to make a turn. He knew he wasn't going to get a clear shot at the tires because of the fog. He fired a shot. The bullet struck metal. He fired another shot and hit the truck again. The truck swerved, hoping to avoid another shot. More bullets pierced metal. The truck swerved from left to right trying to make itself a harder target.

Finally, the truck reached Laguna Boulevard and turned. The man with the shotgun took aim and rapid fired rounds into the lower half of the vehicle. They were aiming for the tires. The truck appeared to be in the clear until the back of the truck dipped. The truck continued on, but the tire tore off, and the rim scraped against the road creating beautiful bright yellow sparks amidst the dark fog.

"How long's he gonna go for?" the man with the shotgun asked.

"It's okay, we got people in both directions," the man with the rifle remarked.

"Should we call them in to go after the truck?"

"No, leave them. We need them in their positions in case this one doesn't work out. Let's go for a walk," the rifleman said.

The truck was pulled over by a patrol car as it approached Franklin Boulevard.

"What's happened here?"

"I got shot at. People were shooting at me. Damn it, it's like we're in the Wild West again."

The officer looked at the wheel and noticed bullet holes on the side and back of the truck.

"Back up, I need back up on the corner of Franklin and Laguna. We've got another attack and shooting of a delivery truck. Officer in danger!" The officer called out to the delivery truck driver, "Come on out! Let me get you outta here. There's a good chance they're coming after us."

The delivery driver jumped out, looked around like a startled cat, and ran to the passenger side of the police car. The police officer stood outside the patrol vehicle's driver side with his gun drawn, looking for any approaching perpetrators. He was conflicted between driving away from a potential onslaught or sticking around and hoping the attackers wouldn't want to shoot at a police officer. *Backup should arrive within a couple of minutes.* The police officer waited.

The truck driver shouted, "Let's go! These guys got lots of guns, big guns."

The police officer became even more nervous, frantically looking around for any sign of trouble. He didn't want the criminals taking goods from the truck. If successful, attacks on delivery trucks would continue to increase, and residents would miss out on crucial deliveries.

"Please, let's go!" the driver yelled again.

The police officer jumped in the car, shut the door, and put the car in drive when he saw police cars with their lights on coming down Franklin. Three cars, one after another, zoomed down the road at highway speeds—sirens blaring and lights flashing. The police officer gained confidence.   The goods inside the truck would be safe. He heard a pop.

Bullets pierced the passenger side of the car, thump, thump, thump. It sounded like hail landed on top of the car. A bullet shattered the passenger glass. The officer ducked. He saw the delivery driver leaning over, mouth and eyes open with blood pouring from his head. He got out of the car and crawled to the front. The shooting was coming from the rear passenger side. The officer fired back in the direction the bullets were coming from. One man hid in the bushes, another was behind a large US Bank sign across Franklin, and the shotgun man ran across the street to surround the car. Boom! Boom! The shotgun fired, shattering both driver side windows. The man with the shotgun stopped firing. The other police cars pulled into the middle of the crossfire, unaware of being surrounded. The shotgun man started firing on the police cars. The officer in the first police car didn't make it out from a shotgun blast to the chest. The officer in the second police car got out and shot across his car at the shotgun man. The officer in the third car did the same.

The original police officer turned his attention to the other two shooters. He could now tell where the shooting was coming from, around the corner by the bushes. But there was another shooter, someone with a long-range rifle. The guy in the bushes stopped shooting. The officer saw bullet sparks coming from the shopping center across the street. They were directed toward the other two police officers.

One officer ducked, while the other got up and shot at the shotgun man. The shotgun man hid behind the streetlight post and fired. The second officer fired back. Suddenly, the second officer fell forward on the hood of the car. Blood and brains splattered across the windshield, shot from behind by the rifleman. The only police officers remaining were the original and the third one.

"More back up needed, police officers down, multiple officers down on the corner of Franklin and Laguna Boulevard!" the original officer shouted into his radio. "He's got a rifle, on the corner across the street," the original officer yelled to the third officer.

"How the hell do we get outta this?" the third officer yelled back.

"I'll take the rifle man and you work on the shotgun." The original officer didn't know what happened to the guy behind the bush. He took quick looks at the intersection, looking for the rifleman. The officer spotted him moving to another location on the same corner. He aimed at the rifleman, hoping to get a clear shot.

The rifleman finally came to a halt, lifted the gun to his face, and aimed. The officer started firing. The guy in the bushes, who disappeared, reemerged behind the original police officer, who was firing at the rifleman. He crept up to the police officer, aimed his pistol, and fired at point blank range.

9

A police car pulled up in front of Angel's Salon. The officer knocked on the boarded door to the salon while peering through the broken opening. He looked down at the shattered glass. "It's Sac PD," he hollered.

Angel looked out from the side and saw the police car parked in the middle of the road.

"Yes, officer. How can I help you?"

"My name's Officer Winston. Is your husband's name Mike?"

She became hysterical. "Yes, yes, why?" she said while pulling the board back to get outside.

"Okay, just wanted to make sure. He and your kids are in my patrol vehicle. They needed a ride to the salon."

"Yes, yes, thank God. I've been waiting on them."

"What are you guys doing here anyway?"

"Officer, people were attacking our home. We called the police several times. They came out once, asked a few questions, and nothing happened. When someone came by and threw one of those cocktails at the house, that's when we knew we had to leave. Thank God it didn't put the house on fire. I came here to set things up and wait for my family."

"You know, I don't know how safe or an effective shelter this place is—"

"It's fine. Believe me, it's fine. As long as we have a place to sleep, and food, and water, we are fine. I just hope things will get better soon so we can go home. I called our insurance company, no one's picking up. I called the gas company… I pay all my bills, you know? Now, our gas is shut off. No one's answering or returning messages."

"My dear, it's a very trying time, and once this passes, things will return to normal. Let me get your family," Officer Winston said.

Officer Winston opened the back door and out came Mike. His eyes were small from a lack of sleep and the brightness of the sun. His goatee looked even whiter, and he walked with a limp to the trunk of the car to get their belongings. He looked as if he'd aged twenty years in the past two days. Three kids came out of the back seat, and his eldest daughter exited the front passenger door. Exhaustion bore over the excitement of being reunited with their mother. Angel rushed out to hug and kiss them, but it wasn't reciprocated.

"Quick, go inside. Say hi to your aunts and find a place to rest, anywhere you want." She went to help Mike get the luggage out. "Where have you guys been?"

"Ah, I don't want to talk about this nonsense," Mike said, which was completely untrue. He wanted to tell the police and their new system off, and the only one who might carry that message to whoever might matter is Officer Winston. "First, the cops pull us over and take us to the police station," Mike said loud enough for the officer to hear. "Then, they leave us there for so many hours, like we're some damn criminals—I mean, it was me and my kids with luggage, for God's sake."

Officer Winston was about to get into the car, when he decided to listen to Mike's venting.

"Then, they freaking take us to the clinic to get tested. I swear to God, if any of my kids get this disease, I will come back and kill every freaking one of them."

"Hey, calm down!" Officer Winston shouted.

"You went to get tested?" Angel asked.

"Yea, God damn it. They take good people and make them sick on purpose. I swear to God, I tell you."

"What were the results?"

"Nothing! Nothing. I told you we are clean people," he told Angel but spoke as if it were directed to the officer. "Then they brought us here, and here we are—no car, no nothing."

"Where's the car?"

"Ma'am," Officer Winston jumped in. "The car had to be left in a parking lot on Jefferson Boulevard. We couldn't take it with us. You can call a tow and have them bring it here or to your house."

"Why do we have to go through that? Why not let him bring the car?"

"Because," Mike answered, "They arrested us. Like we're the criminals. No wonder people get away with crap, because the police are wasting their time with good people. They're not looking for the real criminals."

"Sir," Officer Winston tried to interrupt.

"No, you're a good officer. You're a good man. The other ones are garbage. You wanna know the truth?" Mike asked. "The truth is, the cops don't want to face the real criminals because there's so many of them now, and they all have these crazy weapons. The world's coming to an end. Look! Angel, we're living in your salon. You said the gas is cut off? Next, it will be the electricity, and then the water. The criminals are running this world, and the police are afraid to face them. So, to make it seem like they are doing their jobs, they run checkpoints, and arrest good people who can't fight back."

Mike pulled the luggage out of the trunk and rolled it into the salon. Angel and Winston looked at each other, speechless.

"Don't tell your story to the aunts," she yelled out to Mike.

"Aunts?" Officer Winston asked.

"Yes, my aunts are in there too. I had to help them."

"Oh, this is not good."

"What? What's not good?" Angel asked.

"Well, this isn't a good place to be. Can you go to someone else's home? No, you can't. We don't want too many people together. Let's see. Look, your husband was right about a lot of things, except the part about not fighting crime. There's a chance one of them might've caught the virus at the clinic—a very small chance, but still a chance. I'm concerned about your aunts, who I presume are elderly?"

"Yeah, most of them are."

"It's up to you guys. I'll be here for a few minutes, if you want to have a discussion with them to see if they want me to drop them off somewhere else, or if you guys will take your chances."

"No, we're okay. We'll take our chances."

"You sure? You didn't ask them."

"They came here because they couldn't take being lonely anymore. They would rather take their chances. Auntie Robbie walked here from her apartment a couple of miles away in the middle of the night to be here with her family. We're good."

Officer Winston went about his way.

Mike helped to re-board the door, but not before he boarded the outside of the glass windows first—a project to release some of the built-up tension.

"Four police officers were killed while on duty on the corner of Franklin and Laguna Boulevard last night responding to a call of yet another attack on a delivery truck. The criminals made away with a lot of goods," Julissa from Channel 31 said as Caleb watched the news from his living room couch.

He heard Sadaka turn the shower on. The water ran without anyone under it. Suddenly, he heard a thumping sound against the wall. Sadaka banged on the bathroom wall to get his attention. Caleb went into the bathroom to see what she needed.

"Why isn't this water getting warm?"

"Not sure. Give it a minute."

"I did. It's been three minutes. Can you do something please?"

Caleb checked to make sure the water was turned completely on hot, and it was. He held his hand under the water. It was cold. The water ran over his hand as he thought.

"The other day I took a shower and it was the same thing."

"Can you check the water heater or something? I already feel like I'm getting sick."

Caleb looked at her for a moment, wondering if she had the virus.

"Hurry!" Sadaka said.

Caleb ran into the garage and checked on the water heater. The hot water pump was plugged in, as was the water heater itself. Caleb scratched his head. He looked underneath to see if the pilot flame was on. It wasn't. He followed the steps listed on the water heater to reignite the flame. It didn't work.

"What are you doing?" Sadaka yelled.

"Trying to get this damn thing to turn on."

He tried the steps over and over to no avail. Caleb played a YouTube video on how to ignite the pilot light for water heaters. He'd already done exactly as described. Caleb ran to the kitchen, passing by the bathroom Sadaka was in.

"What are you doing?" she yelled.

"Honey, please. I'm trying to figure out why the flame under the water heater isn't lighting up."

"Fix that later. Just bring me some boiling water."

Caleb went to the kitchen to test the stove top. It clicked but wouldn't ignite either. He tried all four sections, none of them worked.

"We have no gas."

"What's taking so long? I just need some boiling water."

Caleb poured water into their electric water boiler as he ran to the living room and flipped the switch on to the fireplace. It didn't turn on.

"Yup, we got no gas."

He got on the phone to the gas company, but the phone kept ringing and ringing until a busy signal ended the rings. The water finally came to a boil. He took it to Sadaka. She had a pail of cold water, mixed the boiling water with it, and used it to pour over herself. "This is how people in poor countries take showers. If they can do it, I can, except, they don't have the boiling water to make their water warm."

"I'm glad you could think that way at a time like this," Caleb said. "Honey?"

"Yes, babe?"

"Never mind. I'll wait for you to come out."

Caleb shut the door. Sadaka sneezed once, twice, and a third time.

"Wow," Caleb said. "We better get that gas going." That's when he remembered something. Caleb ran to check on the thermostat and increased the temperature. Nothing came on. He waited a few minutes and busied himself with the dishes, washing them using cold water. After cleaning a few cups and plates, he still didn't hear the heater come on. He went to the thermostat—still nothing. "Damn gas company. What the hell is going on there?" Caleb checked online to make sure he was dialing the right number. The number was the same, but no one answered.

"This is Julissa from Channel 31 News, reporting live from the inside of my home. Stay home, everyone."

Caleb turned the TV off.

***

Ishmael grew tired of staying in the same room hour after hour while Pele played video games. He asked Pele to step in and be on the lookout.

"Don't worry, bro. We'll hear the truck when it comes," Pele said.

"What do you mean, 'the truck?' We have to watch for anything suspicious," Ishmael replied. "Get over here and take a turn."

Pele got up and sat in Ishmael's chair. Ishmael lay on the ground, picked up the video game remote, and played for a few minutes before dozing off. Pele heard a rumbling coming from a high-revved engine. He couldn't see the vehicle, but knew it was a truck—and it was coming fast. Ishmael woke to the engine sound. Pele looked out the window for the truck.

"Sit down," Ishmael said. "You'll give us away."

Pele moved to the side but kept an eye on the road. A delivery truck came to a sudden stop right in front of the house they watched. The driver ran out, pulled out a couple of long packages, and rushed them to the front door. He looked under the welcome mat, took the envelope, and stuffed it in his back pocket. He retrieved a couple more boxes and set them beside the others. Just as he headed back for the truck, a neighbor came out of his house.

His face was flushed red, hands balled into fists, headed for the truck.

"What the hell is wrong with you? There are kids in this neighborhood!" the neighbor yelled.

"Yeah, I know. I'm in a hurry," the driver replied as he headed for the driver seat.

"You come here like that next time, I'll show you a hurry."

Someone opened the door to the home that received the delivery. He eyed the neighbor, and the neighbor eyed him back.

"Tell your delivery boys to slow down next time," the neighbor said. "What the hell they delivering to you every day anyway?"

The guy pulled the boxes into the house and closed the door.

"That exchange is all we need to inspect the house," Pele said.

"What exchange?" Ishmael made it to the window with bloodshot eyes.

"The driver made a delivery, and took an envelope from under the mat. It looked like a rocket launcher could fit into those boxes."

"Probably long-range rifles," Ishmael said.

"Let's go and get a warrant."

"Don't rush out," Ishmael said. "We don't wanna give ourselves away last minute and make them suspicious."

10

Pari's temperature rose to 101. Caleb and Sadaka were distraught.

"I think I should stay in a hotel for a little while," Sadaka said.

"If she has it, it's too late. And going anywhere else won't matter for me either. Either I have it, or I won't get it at this point."

"I've stayed in the other room since I've been here. How could it be?"

"We don't know if it's the virus, or a regular cold, or the flu, but you haven't been looking good lately," Caleb said.

"But I don't feel sick. I mean, my throat hurts every now and then, but that's all."

"Have you taken your temperature?"

"No. Here, let me see that," she asked for the thermometer Caleb held. Sadaka took her temperature—it was ninety-nine. "Not bad," she said. "Close enough to normal. We have to watch her closely, make sure she doesn't get other symptoms."

Caleb shook his head. He understood but felt sick to his stomach. It showed on his face, and he had a grimace of pain and uneasiness in his abdomen.

"It'll be okay, honey. Don't worry," Sadaka said. "At least it's not as bad as what's happening in South Sac," she said as a social media notification pinged her phone.

"You mean Natomas?"

"Natomas? What happened there? No, I'm talking about South Sac."

"What's happening in South Sac?" Caleb asked as he curled Pari in his arms and sat on the couch. He gave sleeping Pari a kiss on her little chin.

"You shouldn't get too close. You don't wanna catch what she might have," Sadaka said.

"I'll gladly take anything she has."

"Oh my God," Sadaka said as she stared at her phone. "Turn on the news. I want to see if this is on TV."

"What?"

"South Sac. A family died in their apartment after the city quarantined all the residents of an apartment complex by force."

"How'd they die?"

"Let me see," she scrolled on her phone. "A fire! They died in a fire. My God!"

"A fire? Forced quarantine? I mean, I know it's against the law, and we could go to jail for being outside, but forced? They locked their doors and windows on them?"

"Some people are saying that this apartment complex had lots of people who didn't follow the quarantine rules, and some were sick, so the police, or the army, forced the people into their homes and welded their doors shut."

"Don't believe that. There's too much fake news out there—too many conspiracies. At one point, many conspiracies were based in reality. Now, everyone's making up a story. You can't believe anything these days. No one's welding anyone's windows and doors."

"I don't know," Sadaka said. "Why would random people be talking about it, including one of my friends, Mayson. She lives in South Sac and said that Mack Road was blocked off by military vehicles."

"Let me see," he leaned into her phone with Pari in his lap. Caleb looked at some of the posts, and then looked away. "I don't understand why they would do that. I don't know. It can't be true." He looked into Pari's sleeping face, enjoying the peace she was in. He didn't want to believe the chaos erupting all around him. Sacramento felt as if it sat atop a volcano that gave several warning signs of an impending doom. How many more of these volcanoes were ready to explode in the United States, and around the world?

Pari coughed, a vicious cough that woke her from the peace.

Caleb called Pari's primary health care provider, in South Sacramento. The phone rang and rang. He placed the phone on speaker while rocking her to sleep. She coughed in Caleb's face, and it was a dry cough that sounded as if it was tearing at the back of her throat. Her eyes opened, and she stared into Caleb's. Caleb saw the enjoyment in her eyes. He loved staring at her just as much as she loved staring at him. Another cough momentarily interrupted her gaze, but as soon as it ended, she went back to looking at him. Caleb kissed her forehead before getting off the couch with her still curled into his arms. He grabbed the car keys from the key holder.

"Where you going?" Sadaka asked.

"To the hospital. I want them to check her. I don't wanna wait until it's too late."

"Why don't you call?"

"You hear my phone? That's the hospital. It's been ringing for over five minutes. No one's picking up the phones anymore. Not the gas company, not the hospital, no one. I hope 911 dispatchers are still answering. I might drive by that apartment complex on the way back home. I know where it is."

"You're not going anywhere but straight to the hospital and back. In fact, I'm coming with you. Let me try and get escort service first."

"No, babe. You stay home, relax. I know what I'm doing. Escort service will take a long time, if anyone's even available."

"But you can't go by the apartment. If you don't promise me, I'm coming with you."

"What's the big deal?" Caleb asked. "It's not like I'll catch anything by driving by."

"It's not just the virus I'm afraid of. It's the people too. Plus, Mayson said the road's blocked off. Last thing I need is for you to get arrested, and they won't know what to do with Pari, and they'll send her to some place where she will get sick. No, you can't go!"

"Okay, okay, I won't go."

"Promise?"

"Yeah, I promise. I'll just drive past Mack Road on the way to the hospital."

"Keep me posted every half hour, please. And, don't forget your phone charger."

Caleb grabbed his charger, slipped on his shoes, and left the house. There was an eerie silence outside, no longer uncommon.

***

"What happened with the warrant?" Ishmael asked Pele.

"Bro, the judge isn't giving out any warrants. He says they're too busy with higher level stuff."

"Like what? We wasted our time investigating that house? They got weapons. This will lead to the bigger picture, weapon smuggling—unless that freaking judge is bought out by whoever's running the show."

"The judge is focusing on is getting approval for a house to house inspection to confiscate weapons. The military's stepping in, and they wanna make sure the citizens aren't armed."

"In Elk Grove?"

"In the entire greater Sacramento region," Pele said. "We need the help from the military. Just the other day, four of our brothers died in your backyard," Pele said.

"I know, I know. That's scary stuff. We have to be careful. Things are getting crazy out there."

"You heard about South Sac, right?"

"Yup, and I went to check out the scene, but the military had the roads blocked off for miles around. They wouldn't even let the police through the checkpoint," Ishmael said.

"When the military steps in, it's getting real."

11

Caleb took the longer route to the hospital. He wanted to pass through Mack Road on his way to see if it was really blocked off by the military. The roadways were open, and the green lights accommodating. He made his way to Mack Road in half the time it normally takes before the quarantine went into effect. There were only a few cars ahead of him when he noticed military vehicles ahead. They came to a stop. Men and women in military attire and machine guns strapped to their chest approached the vehicles. One of the military personnel approached Caleb's car.   She gestured for him to lower his window as she stood six feet back.

"Where you headed?"

"To the hospital."

"You'll have to take a detour."

"What's going on here?   Why's the road blocked off?"

"Military business.   We're trying to help keep order and protect everyone," the solider said.

"By doing what?   I mean, I'm just curious as to what's going on."

"Sir, you'll have to take the detour."

Caleb knew when anyone started to address him with the word "sir", when they didn't mean it out of respect, meant the conversation was headed south. He raised his hand to thank her and made a U-turn.

Caleb made it to the hospital.   This time, there were dozens of cars ahead of him, all parked and waiting their turn to talk to the entry point attendant. Caleb took a look at Pari in the car seat. She stared out the window, completely quiet and relaxed. She didn't look sick. Caleb took her temperature—102.5. He was happy, however, that she didn't appear bothered by the increasing temperature. He got out of the vehicle to stretch, when he saw the hospital's parking lot. Caleb froze. *This parking lot made Wymarck look like Disney World. In fact, it looked like we were in a losing war.* Tents were propped up everywhere, as far as the eye could see, and medical specialists with full protective gear and clothing walked in and out of tents. *If this was the scene out here, what did it look like inside the hospital?*

Caleb sent a message to Sadaka, "Looks like we're going to be here for a while." He tagged the message with a picture of the parking lot.

"Sir, I need you back inside your vehicle," another person in military attire said.

This soldier didn't have a machine gun strapped to his chest. Nonetheless, he looked and sounded intimidating. Caleb went inside the car and waited.

Someone else in full head coverings and a mask went from car to car. With a tablet in hand, she asked questions and spent a few minutes with each vehicle. To the side, there was a sign that read, "Tune to station 99.1 KDST for the latest hospital messaging updates." Caleb tuned in. It was the hospital's messaging system.

"…unless your situation is a true emergency, we advise returning home and providing self-care. Hospital staff are stretched thin. Wait times are hours long. Hospital beds for COVID-19 patients are full. Unless you're dying, or an ambulance brings you in, there's no guarantee on when you'll be triaged…"

Caleb turned the radio off. He didn't want to listen to the information. He wanted to talk to the person going from car to car, who might take Pari in. Pari was his life, and he couldn't risk any possibilities.

Two hours and several messages back and forth with Sadaka passed before the person finally made their way to Caleb's car.

"What are you here for?" she asked.

"Nothing with me, I'm fine. It's my daughter in the back. Her temperature's been climbing, and she has a dry cough. It sounds horrible."

She opened the back door to check on Pari.

"She's so adorable. She looks so relaxed."

The specialist took Pari's temperature, "103."

"It was just at 102.5 a couple hours ago, and before that it was 101 at home."

"Sounds like it's climbing fast. I could tell you to take her home and give her over the counter fever reducers, but that'll likely mean the virus will still be with her. The body's reaction to fight things that don't belong inside of us is to raise its temperature to kill the invader off. But with the continuing rise in her temperature, we'll want to keep an eye on it and help prevent it from getting too high."

Caleb felt a ton of bricks come off his shoulders. He couldn't believe what he heard. He thought he'd be told to go home and watch her. "I really appreciate this," he said.

"Oh, no problem. Anything for a beauty like her. I love her lashes," she said while typing something into the tablet. "Someone is going to be here to take her in real soon."

"I can't drive inside and take her in myself?"

"Oh no. We don't allow vehicles inside anymore. There's no space to park, apart from emergency vehicles. The rest of the parking lot is filled with tents of COVID-19 patients."

"Will she be in one of those tents?"

"No, this beautiful girl's going inside to be under special care," she said with a smile that could only be seen by the squinting of her eyes. "Wait here. I have to go and triage the cars behind you."

"Ok, thank you."

Caleb watched in silence as he handed Pari over to two other hospital employees wearing the same protective gear.

"She's so beautiful," one remarked. "What's her name?"

"Pari," Caleb said with sadness and concern.

"We'll take good care of Pari, won't we? We have your information and will provide updates as they come in. You'll be allowed back here once she is ready to go home, or unless we need you back for any other reason. Make sure to answer your phone while your precious daughter is with us. The numbers that might ring to your phone can be different, as people are using their cell phones and hospital phones to make calls. Apart from that, no one's allowed inside the hospital."

"Okay," Caleb said without taking his eyes off of his daughter.

The staff walked off with Pari. They followed behind another staff member who pushed a wheelchair with an elderly man. Caleb watched, hopeless, frustrated, and sad that he wasn't allowed to accompany his daughter. He looked around and saw others being carried off from their cars into the hospital, each person without their loved one to accompany them. *What if these people were pretending to be staff, only to kidnap babies? What if I never see Pari again? This could easily be a scheme, and there's no way of verifying. No one answers the phone, so calling the hospital to confirm is useless. But, why would they be rolling in an elderly man, and another sick woman on a gurney? What benefit would there be in kidnapping them? They can't all be in on the kidnapping of Pari, no! This was the hospital's new process because of the worsening situation with the virus. When will this thing go away? Why can't I be with Pari? Nothing makes sense anymore! And if all this madness was created for the micro-chipping vaccine that I heard about on television, then...* Tears welled up in his eyes. His heart ached at seeing his helpless daughter's head bobbing up and down as the hospital staff walked further away. His chest tightened at the helplessness that he felt about protecting his daughter, at not knowing when he'd see her again, at the thought that she might not survive this ordeal, at the idea that she might not carry the virus and will catch it in the hospital. Caleb slammed his fist on top of the hood as tears poured from his eyes. He sobbed like a baby.

"Sir, you need to move your vehicle," the apathetic guard said as he returned.

Caleb wanted to take his frustration out on the guard. *Why can't he be more compassionate at a moment of such pain?* Caleb eyed him and noticed the size of his neck and forearms. The guard looked like a beast. Caleb didn't stand a chance in a confrontation. Besides, the guard carried a gun in his belt. It was a hectic and chaotic time, and he didn't want to add to the madness, which might end up with him hurt or in jail. *No, the guard's just doing his job. If someone empathetic were in his place, the people would run amuck.* Caleb understood the guard's necessary demeanor.

"Sir!" the guard yelled. "Your vehicle has got to go. I won't say it again. Ma'am, you too, move your vehicle, now!"

Caleb gritted his teeth. He didn't appreciate being yelled at like a child. For a moment, he forgot about Pari. He quickly got inside and drove off.

***

Officers Ishmael and Pele teamed up and convinced the sergeant to have them do the inspections for the part of Elk Grove in which the house they watched was in.

Officers Soraya and David Quaid were on the other side of the street going door to door. They each had a printout of the homes with registered guns, but they knew there were many residents who had unregistered weapons, and they needed to be tactful about retrieving that information to get those weapons.

"Pele, that house is three blocks down. They're gonna see us soon and hide their weapons," Ishmael said.

"Don't trip, if that's what's going on in there, there's no way they can hide everything so fast. We'll check every nook and cranny till we find them. Let's clear these guys out first."

Pele knocked on the door. "Elk Grove PD. Open up please."

Someone looked through the peep hole. Whispering took place behind the door. Pele heard the whispering, so he knocked again, harder. "Open up, this is Elk Grove PD."

The door opened.

Ishmael heard shouting from behind him across the street.

Officer Soraya yelled, "If you don't have anything to hide, you don't have to worry. Next time, I won't be so nice," she walked across the lawn to the next house with David trailing her.

"Bunch of fatherless, low-class people," David said.

"Fatherless? Never heard that before," Soraya said.

Ishmael entered the home right behind Pele.

"We didn't do anything," a short, thin, East Asian man said.

"No, you didn't. Everything is okay. We're just looking for guns," Ishmael said.

"Guns? I no have any guns."

"You don't have any guns?"

"No, no guns."

A lady, the same size as her husband, followed Pele to the kitchen. "How can I help you?"

"Nothing, just looking around. We're collecting guns. You have any guns?"

"No, I don't know," she said, not understanding the officer.

Her husband's voice began to escalate with Ishmael. He turned his attention to his wife and left Ishmael at the entryway. They spoke to each other. It was fast and furious.

"Please, go. No guns," the man shooed off Pele.

"I go when I want to go," he said.

"Pele, let's go.   They don't have anything."

"Na man, these people always got at least a pistol. They weren't persecuted in their countries only to come here and be unarmed," Pele turned to the man, "Where's your gun?   I know you have one."

"We have no GUNS! I know what gun is. You go, now!"

"Pele!" Ishmael yelled.

"If I find out you're lying to me, I will come back here and arrest you."

"Okay, okay, no problem. You arrest me. Thank you. Bye-bye," the man said, happy just to have them leave.

The door slammed behind the officers, followed by loud, aggressive chatter.

"I'm telling you, he's got a gun," Pele said. "If the military finds that gun, it's our asses."

"Let's move on. I'm more concerned about that house. I say we go straight there and forget about the door to door. We go there first, check them out, and then come back to where we left off."

"That's not a bad idea," Pele agreed. "Let's clear the last house on this block, and then we'll check those guys out."

"Open up, Elk Grove PD," Pele said.

The door immediately opened. A guy wearing a disposable mask let them in. "How can I help you, officer?"

"We're going door to door and confiscating guns," Pele gave him a chance to come clean before letting him know a gun was registered to this address.

"Confiscating guns? What about our second amendment rights?"

"Your guns will be replaced by soldiers with bigger guns, so your rights aren't technically being taken away."

The man tried to speak, but Pele continued, "The guards who'll be assigned to protect your neighborhood do not feel comfortable being surrounded with people who have guns. Therefore, to ensure their safety, we have to confiscate all guns before they arrive."

"You know, the right to bear arms is a right every citizen has to protect themselves against any threat, and it doesn't include the military or other law enforcement agency replacing our guns. This isn't right."

"Right or wrong, I'm not here for a debate, but to follow orders. Where's your gun?"

"Of course you know I have a gun, because I got mine legitimately—I registered my gun like a law-abiding citizen. Now, because I am law-abiding, I'll have my rights stripped from me, whereas the thugs and gangsters who have unregistered weapons will go on and keep theirs." The man went to his room.

"I gotta follow you," Pele said.

Ishmael stayed by the front door.

"No problem, you can follow me." The man lifted his mattress but didn't touch the gun.

"Thank you. You know how we operate," Pele said. He took the gun and asked, "Where's the ammunition?"

"Under the bed, but be careful because the gun is loaded."

"Loaded, huh? I thought you said you were law abiding?"

"I am. That doesn't mean I have to follow every ridiculous rule some idiot decides to make up. If someone broke into my house and my ammunition was stored in another room and my gun was empty, how would that help me? The least you could do for us, officer, is to appeal to the idiots who make these rules. Get them to make rules that apply to real life. I understand the restrictions on assault rifles and military grade stuff, I understand that, but this is beyond ridiculous."

Pele didn't argue, not because he didn't want to but because he agreed with every word the man said. He took the ammunition, the gun, emptied the gun, and dumped everything into a bag. He walked back through the hallway and to the front where Ishmael waited.

"So this is it? All hell is breaking loose around us, and I'm left defenseless. This is our United States?"

Pele didn't say anything and continued to the front door.

"Thank you, officer," the man said politely.

Pele gestured for Ishmael to exit. Ishmael left the house. Pele reached for the door, turned around and saw the helpless look on the man's face. He handed the bag back to him. The man took the bag, smiled, and shook his head in gratitude to Pele. Pele closed the door.

"What'd you do with the stuff?" Ishmael asked.

"Gave it back, let's go."

Ishmael stopped. "The hell you mean, 'gave it back?' What happened to 'it's our asses?'"

"I know him," Pele said. "Not trying to take a registered weapon away from someone I know."

"You know him?" Ishmael asked, knowing Pele was lying.

"Yeah, man. Let's go to that house," Pele tried to change the subject. He looked back and saw officers Soraya and David coming out of another house. "Soraya," Pele called out. They walked into the middle of the street. "That house on the corner, three blocks down, we're gonna check that out first and then come back here. That's the house we were on a stakeout for, and if they see us going door to door, we'd basically be prepping them for the visit."

"That makes sense," Soraya said. "You need backup?"

"Probably not, but better safe than sorry, if you guys don't mind."

"No, I don't mind at all. I think it's better if we back you up. You never know. Better to have us and not need us, you know?"

Pele waved Ishmael down, and they walked toward the house. Soraya informed David of the plans.

"Why can't you let them do their thing? I want to finish our side so we can go on to the next neighborhood," David said.

"They need our help. We're going to help them. Let's go. We're not going inside, just watching their backs."

"I wasn't going inside anyway. Make it quick," David demanded.

***

"Her temperature's at 104, and her breathing is shortening," Nurse Yasmeen called out to Aisha, the CNA, to enter notes in the computer. "It's getting harder for her to breathe. We need to get her on a ventilator," Yasmeen said.

There were no rooms available to place Pari in. Yasmeen kept Pari in a bed by her side at the nurse's station and ordered for a portable ventilator to be brought to her.

***

Ishmael's heart pounded as they approached the house. He drew his gun, expecting a bad outcome.

"What you doing, bro? They're not trying to go to war with four cops. Put your gun away."

"Don't worry, Ishmael. We got your back," Soraya said.

Ishmael looked back and wondered who "we" were, as David stayed across the street and watched.

Pele knocked on the door, "Open up, Elk Grove PD."

Ishmael heard sounds in the backyard come to a sudden silence.

****

"Intubate her," Yasmeen instructed Aisha. The CNA placed tubes inside Pari's nostrils. She turned her head from left to right and started crying.

"It's okay, sweetheart," Yasmeen placed her hands over Pari's shaking arms. She rubbed the back of Pari's soft hands to help her calm down. As soon Aisha finished inserting the tubes, Pari calmed. Nurse Yasmeen placed Pari's pacifier back in her mouth and wiped a tear away from the side of her face. She turned the ventilator on.

"Should I text her father?" Aisha asked.

"No. Don't worry him. Let's get everything under control and give him good news when it's time."

***

"Elk Grove PD—open the door," Pele yelled. "Now, you got me nervous," Pele said to Ishmael.

Ishmael placed his gun back into the holster but left the holster unlocked. He was on edge, and his heart was still racing. The door cracked open.

"Yes? How can I help you?"

"We need to search the house for guns and weapons. Everything must be confiscated before the military arrives."

"Umm, we don't have any guns," the guy said.

"Can we come in and check?"

"You got a warrant?"

"Yea, I do," Pele pulled it out. "It's for the entire city of Elk Grove."

"Hold on," the guy said as he went to shut the door.

"No, we can't hold on," Pele said as he inserted his hand through the opening. He didn't want to take any chances with them hiding the guns or preparing for something worse. Pele forced himself in. "You saw the warrant, now it's illegal to keep us out."

The guy moved back. Pele entered. Staring back at him was a family—men, women, and a couple of kids.

***

"Her temperature's still going up. It's now at 104.5. We're gonna need a fever reducer. She's sweating pretty badly. Get her hooked to an IV," Nurse Yasmeen instructed. "Hi, baby. Hi, Pari. You're such a good patient. You're such a good girl. You're handling this better than anyone I know, even the toughest of them all," Yasmeen said in a comforting tone.

Pari smiled and turned her head sideways. Aisha inserted the needle into Pari's arm, causing her to cry. As soon as the poke was complete, her crying stopped. Aisha finished hooking up the IV.

"She's such a good girl," Aisha said. "I think she needs a diaper change."

She removed her diaper, which was full of diarrhea. "I'm glad we got her hooked to the IV, otherwise she'd be in trouble from dehydration."

***

"Wanna remove the children?" Pele asked.

Officer Ishmael's commanding size stepped into the doorway, taking up the entire entrance. The family simply stared and watched.

"Honey, take the children upstairs," a middle-aged man with a thick mustache said. "What's this about?"

One of the ladies took the two children by their hands. "We're gonna leave," she said.

"No, you'll stay here. No one's leaving, not yet," Pele said.

Ishmael looked at everyone's eyes. He saw the same look of concern across all their faces. One by one, each person made their way toward the back of the house, away from the police and the conflict.

"Take the kids upstairs, honey," the middle-aged man said.

The lady led them by their hands upstairs.

"We're here to confiscate any weapons you may have. It's nothing personal, it's happening to the entire city of Elk Grove."

"For what?" the man asked.

"Because the army will be here soon to protect the residential areas from the criminals taking over the streets, but they can't have everyone around them with guns. They don't know who's who," Pele said as he looked the man in the eyes and felt uneasy.

"My boy told you already, we don't have guns."

"I didn't ask about guns, I said weapons, but since you mentioned guns, bring them out."

"Huh, this is funny," the man said as he rubbed his mustache. "To think we would need to defend ourselves against criminals, here comes the po-lice to disarm everyone. Officer, how you think people gonna defend themselves when the bad guys have weapons and the people don't? You see the crap that's going on out there?" he pointed. "What you guys doing, ain't right. You should be out there, fighting them, not in here disarming us."

Officer Soraya squeezed her way past Ishmael. "Listen, guys. Just do what the officer says so we can move on and do the rest of our job. Don't complicate things. We don't want to take everyone to jail."

"Jail?" the man smirked. "Na, you ain't taking no one to jail."

Ishmael's heart pace picked up again. The man wasn't going to be bullied.

Ishmael nudged Soraya, and she went back outside.

"What's going on in there?" Officer David asked.

"The fatherless people are being difficult," Soraya said.

"Soraya," David said. "Look over there. Isn't that your brother, Joe's car?"

12

Soraya pounded rapidly on Sam's door. Sam was one of Joe's friends. Sam invited Joe and other friends on a weekly basis for card games, food, and chatter. Soraya thought Joe stopped attending these gatherings. Sam opened the door.

"Is Joe here? His car's parked outside your house."

"Uh, uh," Sam searched for words.

Soraya saw cards littered around in the living room. "Can you let me in to see if he's here?"

"Uh, he's here," Sam came clean. He didn't want to get caught lying to his friend's sister, and a police officer at that.

Joe came out from behind the living room wall.

"I can't believe you, Joe. What are you doing here?" Soraya asked.

"Don't tell mom. I don't want her to worry," Joe said.

"I have to so she can yell at you, so you don't do anything like this again. This is so dangerous. I can't believe my smart brother would do something like this. Hey!" she yelled at Sam.

"What's wrong with you guys? Don't you know about the quarantine? You guys think this is a joke? Ever since this virus started, you've been taking it as a joke. Now look at what's going on, and still you're…" Soraya noticed cards all over the floor. "You guys playing your stupid card games?" She turned her attention back to Joe. "I can't believe this. Get in your car, now! Go straight home. I'm gonna call mom and tell her you're on the way back."

"Soraya, I'm going. But I think it's a bad idea if you say anything to them."

"You know what? Go straight to my house and stay in the garage till I get home. I don't want you getting mom and dad sick with your filthy friends. How did you drive here anyway? No patrol cars saw you?"

"Soraya, what are you doing?" Officer David called out. "Get over here. We need you. It's getting bad over here."

***

"Her temperature's going down. It's back to 103.5, but her breathing's still shallow," Aisha said.

"It's not shallow, it's restricted—she's having a hard time breathing," Yasmeen clarified.

"The last time this happened to someone, we lost them," Aisha said with concern.

"We're not losing her. We're not losing this one as long as you follow my instructions. Take her down to ICU. I'll be right there. And don't come back here until I get there."

Aisha rolled Pari's bed to the elevator and down to the Intensive Care Unit. Yasmeen arrived shortly thereafter and spoke to the head nurse. "I need to be here to assist with this baby girl, Pari. Her situation is very sensitive, and I can't risk losing her. I need to stay here with her, and another one of your nurses can take my place on the floor above, just until I get her out of here."

"You know I can't allow that. Everyone's scheduled to be in a specific place for a reason," the head nurse said.

"I know you can't allow it, but I also know you don't have to report it. There's way too much going on for anyone to notice and make a big stink over it. Again, as soon as she's recovered, I'm going back with her and I'll send your nurse back. I've already informed my unit, and they're expecting someone else."

The head nurse didn't know what to do. She was being pulled in different directions, and now she had to deal with this decision. She noticed one of her nurses on his cell phone again, probably playing games.

"Tony," she waved him down.

He put the phone in his back pocket and came over. "It was my mother. She hasn't been feeling so well lately," Tony said.

It was hard to tell these days who was lying and who wasn't because there was so much sickness around, so she held her tongue. "I need you on the third floor, station C for the remainder of your shift."

"Oh, you mean out of ICU?" he asked with excitement in his voice.

"Yes, we have someone else who needs to be here for a while."

"Sure thing. Aye-aye, Captain. Let me grab my stuff, and I'll be on my way."

Tony ran off. Yasmeen thanked the head nurse and looked for Aisha. She saw her in a room that already had another patient. She pulled the curtain that split their side from the other patient, "Always put up as many barriers as possible. You can stay with me if you can find a replacement, or you can return to your station, Aisha."

"I'll return to my station. I've got a few patients who are looking forward to seeing me."

"Go on, honey. Go and spread your magic to as many people you can."

***

"No one wants to take anyone to jail. We only have a job to do, and we'll be outta your hair. What's your name, by the way?" Pele asked.

"My name? Just call me Z."

"And my name's Pele. It's nice to meet you," Pele said as he tried to connect with Z.

"Pele, I like that name," Z said. "I think you know that things are getting bad out there, really bad. If I had any guns, I think it's best they stay. If I don't have any guns, like I say, then I don't have any to give. Officer—"

Ishmael coughed. Pele knew Ishmael was becoming frustrated at how Z was leading and taking over the conversation. He didn't want anything to happen, no arrests, no trouble, but he knew Ishmael wasn't going to stand for Z's tone any longer. They were the police. They had the badges and guns, ready to be used if necessary. They had the authority. Pele heard Ishmael take in a deep breath.

"Officer, like I said, there's a lot of crap going on in the streets that you need to pay attention to. You shouldn't be going from home to home, taking people's guns. That ain't right."

Pele became upset, but his gut feeling was not to challenge him. He wanted to talk his way through this no matter how long it took.

"Hey!" Ishmael called out. He puffed his chest out, and his arms spread out like wings as he made his way past Pele. Pele grabbed his arm to try and hold him back, but Ishmael barely felt it. He pulled off his mask and was face to face with Z, looking down at him. Z didn't bother looking up at Ishmael. He stared into Ishmael's chest, as if he was still looking at Pele. "Knock it off and listen to the man," Ishmael demanded. "We're here for the guns."

The other family members made their way back into the background, concerned about what might happen.

"We know you guys got weapons. We know about the deliveries. We know about paying the drivers," Ishmael continued as Z's face flushed red." We've been on a stakeout of your place."

"Heyyy, ain't you that officer that came here the other day?" Z said as he moved to the side and resumed talking to Pele. "So, you guys been on a stakeout, huh?"

"Stop wasting our time and give up the weapons!" Ishmael demanded.

Pele reached for Ishmael again. He tugged at his arm. Ishmael turned around. Pele was trying to get him to stand down.

"Na, forget that!" Ishmael yelled. "These punks ain't gonna have their way with us, not today."

Pele became nervous and frustrated with Ishmael. He didn't want a confrontation, but Ishmael rubbed salt into the wound.

"You guys want guns?" Z asked.

Pele's heart pumped a thousand times a second.

***

"She's stable, but still very symptomatic," Yasmeen replied to the head nurse after inquiring about Pari.

"You know, I could get used to your presence around here in exchange for Tony," the head nurse smiled.

"I can't handle the pressure you guys are under. It's very intense in here, and the only reason I'm here is because I'm not letting another tiny soul slip from my grip because of the virus. This is personal."

The head nurse put her hand over Yasmeen's shoulder as Yasmeen held her hand over Pari's palm. The head nurse said, "Nothing's guaranteed in life, not even life. He brings life and He takes it when it's time. Don't beat yourself up. The virus is just an excuse. If it's not the virus, it's cancer, or a car accident, or something else."

"I know, but we have to try our best before giving up, and I'm giving it all to this little angel. She's special. There's something magical about her."

***

"Why don't you guys get goin'? Let's end this conversation on a positive," Z said.

"You don't get it," Ishmael said as he grabbed Z by the collar of his shirt.

Z knocked his hand away and pulled out his pistol from behind him. Pele aimed his gun. Ishmael pulled out his pistol, and three others from behind Z aimed their guns.

"I'll die before I let you take our guns and leave us defenseless to anyone who wants to prey on us!" Z said.

Hearts raced on both sides. No one wanted this.

"I suggest you leave and pretend this never happened," Z said as he held his gun aimed at Ishmael's head, while Ishmael kept his on Z's chest.

"Everyone, calm down," Pele said. "Nothing needs to happen here."

"That's right, if you leave!" Z yelled.

David approached the house as he heard the commotion. "Soraya, damn it. Get over here!"

Soraya saw the seriousness in David's face. "Get out of here," she shouted to Joe before rejoining the others. "What the hell is going on here?" she yelled. Soraya drew her gun.

David aimed his gun from the middle of the road. "I told you we shouldn't have been involved with this," he whispered to Soraya from behind.

"And you would leave them to fend for themselves?"

"Drop your weapons, all of you," Ishmael ordered. "Do you want to add cop killing to your records?"

"We'll add cop killin' to our records if you're willing to leave us stranded to die defenseless," Z said.

"You're not defenseless!" Ishmael roared. "The army will be here to protect you, to guard the neighborhoods. Which part of what he said," Ishmael referred to Pele, "didn't you understand? Now drop your weapons!" Ishmael noticed the grip on Z's gun tighten. He wasn't going to lower his gun, and he wasn't going to give up their weapons. Rifles and shotguns were aimed at them from the kitchen behind Z. Men and women kept aim. They were all ready to fight and die to the end. Z was clearly the leader, and whatever he decided would be followed by the others. Z made his decision, and now it was up to the police to make theirs. Pele wanted to end the confrontation, not from a cowardly stance, but he realized they were outgunned. They could leave and return later with a greater force, but Ishmael couldn't allow civilians to get away with making the police cower. He looked into Z's eyes one last time to see if there was a glimmer of hope, an ounce of regret. Instead, the look in Z's eyes was that of pure determination. Ishmael looked at the people standing in the other room. They were robots ready to follow Z's lead. Ishmael kicked Z in his chest. Z's arm flung straight up as he tried to catch his balance, and the first bullet went into the ceiling. Z fell backward into his family, and they were unable to shoot. Ishmael shot at the crowd as he ran out of the house. Pele shot at the family and struck one of the men holding a rifle. Ishmael continued to shoot from outside the house, allowing space for Pele to exit. As Pele ran out, the group regained their composure and started firing. Shotgun rounds sprayed the exit, striking Ishmael on the side of his face. He ran further back and noticed Pele stopped. He fell forward like a falling tree, face smacking against the concrete before any other part of his body.

"PELE!" Ishmael yelled as he hid behind the corner of the house. Everyone inside the house stopped shooting as soon as the police officers were out of sight. They didn't come out of the house to engage in further confrontation. Two of them went to the backyard to keep an eye out for any police trying to jump their fence. One went upstairs to see what the police were up to. Two others, including Z, remained downstairs, guns aimed at the door.

"They left," a voice from upstairs called out. "They're gone."

"Pack the essentials, we have to get out of here," Z said. He went to close the front door, but not before setting eyes on Pele's face that hugged the ground, surrounded by a pool of blood. "I told you guys to leave. You can't come in here and take our right to defend ourselves. We have the right to defend ourselves," Z spoke to Pele's dead body as he tried to comfort his own soul by justifying the murder. He took in a deep breath, and continued, "They call me Z because that's the last thing you'll see when you mess with me."

***

"Hi. May I speak to Caleb?" Aisha said.

"Yes? Is this the hospital?"

"Yes. My name is Aisha. I'm working with Nurse Yasmeen."

"How's Pari? How's my girl?"

"I wanted to let you know that her symptoms worsened since last night, and she's in the ICU right now."

Caleb dropped the phone before taking in another word.

"Sir? Sir? Caleb?"

Caleb walked out of the house. Sadaka picked up his phone. "Hello?"

"Yes, who's this?"

"Sadaka, his wife, Pari's mom. What happened to my baby?" she cried.

"Ma'am she's in the ICU."

Sadaka fell to her knees. "How's she doing?" she asked.

"Not well. Her temperature is lower than before, but still high, and she can't breathe fully on her own."

"She can't breathe? Why? What's happening to her? She was fine just a day ago. SHE WAS FINE JUST A DAY AGO!" Sadaka cried. "WHAT'S HAPPENING TO MY DAUGHTER, TO MY PARI?" she cried.

Caleb walked off into the bandit-run streets. He became a walker amongst walkers. He was going to walk as long and far as he could until his legs would give out or until his daughter was better.

***

Officer Ishmael set his badge and gun on the Captain's desk after being told they would not send a force out to Z's home. The Captain said the military would handle law and order in every neighborhood, and that the police were no longer equipped to handle such issues.

Ishmael went home to his wife and children. He told them what happened, and about the wound on his cheek. He paid respects to Officer Pele's parents.

"I'm sorry I couldn't save your son," Ishmael cried.

Pele's father spoke, "I told him about this line of work. I told him not to get into it, but he insisted. We were poor, and he wanted to make ends meet, so he picked up on police work. He became damn good at it too."

"He did—one hell of a cop," Ishmael said.

Pele's mom watched and listened from the other room. She couldn't stop crying for a moment to get a word in.

"I couldn't save him," Ishmael repeated, "But he died saving us." He took a deep breath. "I left the force. I quit."

"Why'd you quit, son?"

"Because I realized how expendable we are. They're not sending anyone to get the bastards who did this, who killed a police officer. If they don't care about us, if they can't protect us, I can't risk my life for them."

"My son was a real martyr. He stayed to defend and protect the people until his last breath—you even said so. A real man stays with the job he values, and knows it's importance because of what he does. Who's going to protect you, or your family, or us, or other people if everyone thinks like you? No one will be around to protect us, and you speak of needing to be protected."

Ishmael lowered his eyes. "I'm truly sorry for what happened." He saw Pele's mom beside herself, and left her alone.

Not only were the police not to return to that house, but they were called off duty and ordered only to protect their immediate neighborhoods. The military were needed to protect businesses, banks, corporations, political offices, and affluent neighborhoods throughout the United States. There weren't enough servicemen and women to help guard and protect all the neighborhoods throughout the country, so no force was ever sent back to Z's neighborhood. The civilians were left to fend for themselves.

COVID-19 extended to 2021 and beyond. It didn't go away like the experts thought. It didn't go on hiatus like the cold and flu. Its contagion rate remained high, and its death count continued to climb month after month.

Z and two of his family members paid their neighbor a visit, the one who yelled at their delivery driver for speeding. He was a nuisance for Z and his family, continuously getting in their business. They shot him at point blank range and decided to hide out in his house in the event the police or military would return. Z was now the alpha in the neighborhood and promised safety to his neighbors, as long as they wouldn't turn against him. The majority of their neighbors were on board with Z, to be the eyes and ears of the neighborhood—to protect and defend against any unwanted intrusion. All except a couple of homes agreed to this pact. Everyone was left alone, as long as they didn't interfere with how Z operated. Z wanted his neighborhood to be quarantined, where everyone stayed in, no one left without his knowing and permission, and no outsiders could enter. As soon as Z found out the

Natonal Guard and police wouldn't return, half of his family went back to their own house, while Z and the others involved in the shootout stayed in the neighbor's house.

Deliveries stopped. Brick and mortars shut down. Online orders mattered no more. News stations stopped reporting after reporters no longer went out to collect stories due to the existing threats. The occasional news that came on was from Washington. Sporadic promises were made that we were winning the war against the virus, that law and order was still stable, and that criminals would be held to the fullest extent of the law.

"Do not lose hope, citizens of the United States. Do not think that criminals will have their way. In the end, they will see the lack of fruit from their actions. Their days are numbered, as is the Coronavirus'. They will see no mercy, not even those from the more liberal states, because every crime committed during this time is considered a federal crime. In the meantime, stay safe by staying in quarantine," the President said.

To be continued…

AUTHOR'S NOTE

COVID-19, how bad is it? How bad will it get?

I have to admit, I'm one who downplayed the virus and its implications at the onset. Since then, I've had to adjust my tune on a few occasions, like someone searching for the right signal on their radio. Regardless of the health and economic outcome of COVID-19, one thing's for certain, it's been a wake-up call for many people around the globe, especially those in developed "first-world" countries.

How dependent are we? How prepared are we? For what? For whatever might have come from this, for whatever might come in the future. For example, many experts in the medical and scientific communities are more concerned with issues such as increasing antibiotic resistance leading to untold deaths from bacterial infections that we won't be able to do anything about.

COVID-19 is an opportunity, like any challenge in life, to test where we stand as human beings. These challenges separate the stuff that falls to the bottom from the cream of the crop. Who will panic and revert inwardly, focusing only on themselves and their immediate family, and who won't allow the panic to consume what makes them human? Who will be amongst those who hoard and turn their garage into a mini market, and who will be those who gave extra toilet paper to a lady who was saddened when she entered a market only to find all the toilet paper was sold out? Who will be those who continue to feed people who are dying from malnutrition and starvation? Who will be amongst those the world needs? Or do we need everyone to stay home and lock their doors until the pandemic goes away?

I'll take this opportunity to thank the supermarket employees, everyone in the delivery realm, essential service providers, emergency personnel, and, last but definitely not least, those in the medical field whose lives are increasingly at risk. These individuals understand the risk and continue to fight to keep us alive. Thank you!

When the pandemic finally ends, we will go back to the way life was, as usual after any atrocity. This means that we don't take lessons from painful opportunities; that we don't learn from history. Or do we? Are our brains wired with revamped blueprinting each time we go through a crisis, something that lingers in our subconscious and helps us make new decisions? Will we think twice before leaving a restroom without washing our hands? I'm no psychologist, but I'll do my best to be a creature of conscious.

KD Storm authored Carson's Garage, a tale
of friendship, love, loyalty, and sacrifice
that defies reason.
Get your copy online or visit
www.KdStorm.com.

KdStorm.com